IMPORTA[NT]

YOU MUST READ THE FOLLOWING BEFORE CONTINUING

Surviving a major zombie outbreak is a challenge many are prepared for but few are ready to face the difficulties of getting around once the country is over-run by a nasty mixture of the walking dead, half-crazed survivors and post-apocalyptic raiders.

The Ministry of Zombies has teamed up with major motoring organisations and industry partners to create a definitive guide to all things 'transport' in a world of the zombies. From foraging at a local supermarket to relocating across the country, survivor transport needs will be varied and complex. But, be assured that Haynes has assembled a crack team of industry specialists, engineers, survivalists and a few others who just turned up for the buffet to consider your 'end of the world' transport needs.

This volume is the most comprehensive survey of transport options post-zombie apocalypse. It includes not only innovative case studies and plans from which you can create your own vehicle but also important insights around key issues such as driving style, other road users and fuel availability after the world ends. We'll review your transport options on land, sea and even in the air, as well as some unpowered solutions which become the last options for the desperate.

In terms of weapons, where the original designers have added firearms accessories to vehicles, these will be shown in the plans. Many of these options can be replaced with home-made weapons if, like many in the UK, you find yourself facing the zombie hordes armed only with a rolled up copy of the *Guardian* and a small fruit peeler.

You should read this book carefully. Many of the suggestions and ideas are radical and you must ensure that any amendments to your vehicles comply with current legal road requirements. For example, it is not currently permitted to affix zombie-slicing chain saws to the sides of your Nissan Micra. The zombie survival transport prepper must be a wily operator, a shrewd dealer and a cool cat. Vehicles are going to be in high-demand when things get tasty. You can't afford to advertise the fully equipped Bug-Out beach buggy in your garage. Be knowledgeable and prepared but be discreet.

A final word – we at Haynes have worked to make this volume as manufacturer neutral as possible. Most well-known international car brands were consulted and involved in our research apart from the Italians. They turned up on the wrong day and missed out on everything. So, occasionally, we'll mention car marques but the truth is there are some fine models out there, many of which can easily be adapted into high-performance post-apocalyptic vehicles.

With the knowledge in this book, a good set of tools, a few hours and a slice of good luck, we hope you'll enjoy many years of happy post-apocalyptic motoring. Time to put the kettle on and open the Hobnobs, we're about to go a little Mad Max on your ass.

Sean T. Page
Ministry of Zombies, Transport Committee

CONTENTS

ZOMBIE SURVIVAL MANUAL

If you're new to zombies, you should refer to the *Zombie Survival Manual*. This transport volume is not intended for those with no knowledge of walking dead or the zombie virus. The two books are designed to complement each other and together provide a comprehensive zombie survival resource for experienced survivalists and those new to zombie survival preparation.

GETTING AROUND IN ZOMBIELAND

In this manual, we interpret 'transport' in the widest possible terms – that's why you'll find detailed schematics of many different forms of transport to carry you and your supplies, from pimped disability scooters all the way up to purpose-designed apocalypse campervans and even ultra light aircraft.

In reality, most zombie preppers have a mix of vehicles depending on their requirements and it is important to consider your own 'end of the world' needs before we delve into the mechanical detail. For example, we are going to assume that you already have a Bug-Out Plan – that is an emergency set of procedures to get you through the zombie apocalypse. Although there are thousands of variants of Bug-Out Plans, they generally fall into one of two categories and the zombie survival community is split over which is best. In the end, it comes down to a personal decision based on your own circumstances.

1) STAYING PUT

Broadly speaking, this means staying either at home or in a nearby location, fortifying it and seeing out the early chaos of the zombie apocalypse by staying off the streets. Typically, preppers opting for this survival strategy will use the Ministry of Zombies 90-Day Survival Plan which involves having 90 days worth of food, water and supplies – the logic being that by sealing yourself and your family off you can escape the violent early phase of an outbreak when desperate survivors and growing numbers of the dead will be trawling our towns and cities for victims.

▶ TYPES OF VEHICLE

KEY FEATURES
BUG-OUT VEHICLE

▶ Built for extensive road trips
▶ Long-range capability (typically in excess of 400 miles on one 'tank')
▶ Mainly defensive armaments
▶ Good storage space for long-term bug-out supplies
▶ Room for the whole crew – could be used as living quarters
▶ Reinforced frontal grill and bull bars to enable the ramming of blocking vehicles
▶ Your vehicle will need off-road capability as apocalypse conditions are rarely perfect.
▶ Blends in. A vehicle stacked with supplies on the roof could be a tempting target.

'I'VE SEEN WHAT HAPPENS TO AN URBAN ENVIRONMENT DURING A ZOMBIE OUTBREAK IN SERBIA. THERE'S A LOT OF TALK ABOUT 'THE OFF-THE-ROAD WINDOW' AND KEEPING YOUR HEAD DOWN. IN REALITY, IT DOESN'T WORK. TO SURVIVE, YOU NEED A WELL-MAINTAINED BUG-OUT VEHICLE TO GET YOU TO SAFE LOCATIONS'
MICK 'FROSTY' HILLS, ZOMBIE SURVIVALIST, EX-SAS TROOPER

2) BUGGING-OUT

A phrase popular in the survival community, it refers to getting all of your family or team and supplies into a vehicle and getting the hell out of Dodge. Preppers preferring this strategy will have an agreed Bug-Out location and a detailed plan of how to get there, be it an off-shore island, an isolated farm or perhaps a large forest. The key factor in bugging-out is how to survive and complete the journey.

▶ The zombie survival community is split down the middle on the subject of staying put or bugging out. You'll find expert sources on the web extolling the virtues of both approaches.
▶ In a recent poll on a zombie survival forum, just over 53% favoured staying in or close to home and this has been the survival orthodoxy for the last few decades.
▶ At the end of the day, a quality vehicle could perform both roles if required.

STAY PUT OR BUG-OUT?

In truth, many preppers mix and match these strategies – they may have a 90-Day Survival Plan set up around the house and also keep a Bug-Out Vehicle (sometimes known as a BOV) close by in case things turn frosty.

Equally, however, from a secure location, you may decide that embarking on a long journey at the height of the crisis is madness and that you only need a Zombie Apocalypse Vehicle (often known as a ZAV) for local foraging and raiding.

It's important not to get too bogged down in the difference between a BOV and a ZAV as to some extent it doesn't make that much difference. What is key is that you develop your transport solutions around your own zombie survival plan. If you plan to stay put then think about a light vehicle for raiding local sites. If you already have an agreed long-term survival location then you need something robust and big enough to get you and your party there, although that's not as simple as it sounds.

KEY FEATURES
ZOMBIE APOCALYPSE VEHICLE

▶ Short to medium range cruiser
▶ Able to hand most road conditions
▶ Designed for combat, with both defence and offensive weapons
▶ Storage space for foraged resources
▶ Well-able to handle any raiders in terms of speed and performance
▶ Could be a standard family car which is adapted once the dead rise
▶ Ensure you have a good stock of consumables and spares
▶ If you have the space and budget, an off-road motorcycle is an ideal secondary ZAV
▶ Remember to keep your vehicle safe during the first weeks of chaos.

'PEOPLE GET HUNG UP ON ALL THE ZOMBIE SURVIVAL TERMS. FORGET BOVS & ZAVS – IF YOU LIVE IN A TOWN OR CITY THE BEST POLICY IS TO STAY PUT AND GET THE RIGHT VEHICLE MIX TO DO THIS. THINK POWERFUL ROAD CRUISER FOR SERIOUS FORAGING AND DEALING WITH BANDITS'

JACK FALLOW, URBAN SURVIVORS FORUM

GETTING AROUND IN ZOMBIELAND

ASSESSING YOUR REQUIREMENTS

Before reading any further or putting a deposit down on an ex-US military Hummer you found on eBay, you should complete a transport needs assessment. For example, if your strategy is to stay put in a well-fortified home for the first 90 days before emerging to forage and loot in the wasteland, then a hardcore battle car might do the job, along with a good stock of fuel and spare parts – ideal for short-range raiding and scaring off the local gangs.

However, if stage one of your plan is to 'head out to the country' then you are going to need a suitable long-distance transport solution – like a coach or a variation of the London Apocalypse Bus detailed later in this volume. Basically, you'll need the capacity to transport you, your group and its supplies across some of the toughest environments. Ensure you consider the size, mix and ability of your party. Will they all be in one location? Review your Bug-Out Route – does it avoid built up areas?

In a survey by *Automotive* magazine, more than 90% of current road users were shown to be poorly prepared and equipped for motoring in the wake of a major zombie outbreak. That's a shocking statistic considering the ongoing work of organisations such as the Ministry of Zombies and the increasing popularity of zombie fiction and television shows. In most cases drivers just failed to grasp the gravity of the end of civilisation – including an associated collapse in law and order.

'IF YOU'RE LOOKING AT HOW TO GET AROUND ONCE THE DEAD RISE, YOU CAN'T AFFORD TO IGNORE WHAT WILL BE GOING ON AROUND YOU. YOU'LL BE FACING THE CHAOS OF A MAJOR VIRAL OUTBREAK, WITH ALL THE DANGERS THAT WILL BRING. SO, THINK IT THROUGH AND PLAN CAREFULLY'
KYE ANDERSON, FOUNDER OF ENDOFDAYS.COM AND EXPERT ZOMBIE PREPPER

GETTING AROUND IN ZOMBIELAND
IMMEDIATE TRAVEL PLANS

It is interesting to note that, in transportation terms, very few in this country are prepared for the zombie apocalypse but just how unprepared are we as a nation? In April 2017, *Automotive* magazine carried out a survey of its readers to find out. They asked, 'The country has been overrun by zombies, what are your immediate travel plans?'

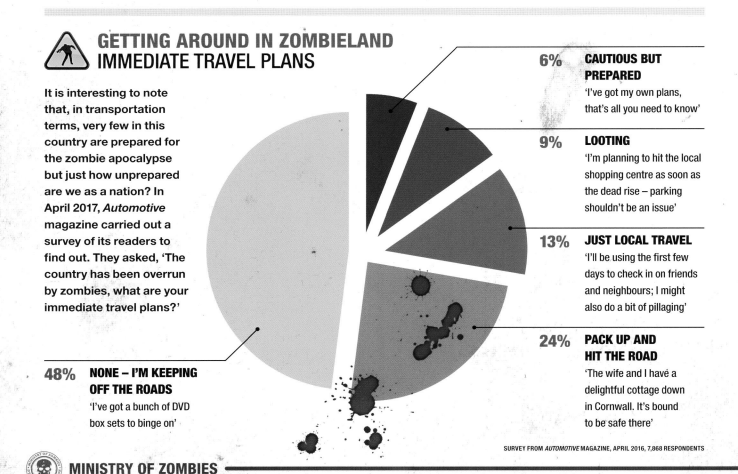

6% CAUTIOUS BUT PREPARED
'I've got my own plans, that's all you need to know'

9% LOOTING
'I'm planning to hit the local shopping centre as soon as the dead rise – parking shouldn't be an issue'

13% JUST LOCAL TRAVEL
'I'll be using the first few days to check in on friends and neighbours; I might also do a bit of pillaging'

24% PACK UP AND HIT THE ROAD
'The wife and I have a delightful cottage down in Cornwall. It's bound to be safe there'

48% NONE – I'M KEEPING OFF THE ROADS
'I've got a bunch of DVD box sets to binge on'

SURVEY FROM *AUTOMOTIVE* MAGAZINE, APRIL 2016, 7,868 RESPONDENTS

THE OFF-THE-ROAD WINDOW

The first few months of a zombie outbreak are often referred to in zombie survival planning circles as the 'Off-the-Road Window'. This term is most relevant for urban survivors and is based on the assumption that the initial chaos and lawlessness of the opening months of any crisis is the ideal time to be hunkered down. Let the unprepared, the newly undead and the crazies battle it out on the street before emerging from your fortified bastion. Keep yourself and your vehicle secure and under wraps.

KEY EVENTS

▶ With your zombie outbreak monitoring systems in place, the moment you suspect a major incident, you need to enact your Bug-Out or Lock-Down Plans. Basically, get to where you need to be quickly before the chaos develops.

▶ Survival psychologists often talk about a 'period of denial' – a time when most of the populace will simply try to carry on as normal despite the growing madness. You'll hear talk of the authorities 'getting on top of the problem' or 'the UN is sending a force'. Even if it's true, you can't take that chance. Your main advantage is knowledge so use it and act quickly.

▶ If you are locking down, try to keep a low profile. You may have the chance to top up on any last minutes supplies but be discreet – don't start a panic by dashing through the supermarket warning about the end of the world.

▶ Finally, once you are where you want to be, whether a Bug-Out Location or your fortified home, run silent and observe. Maybe the authorities will win back control, maybe the off-the-road window will last for months. You need to prepared for every scenario. Be adaptable, be alert and ready to act.

'THE IMMEDIATE AFTERMATH OF A ZOMBIE OUTBREAK IS NOT THE TIME TO BE STOCKING UP ON SUPPLIES AND CRUISING THE STREETS. THOSE OF US PREPARED FOR THE END MUST BE ON GUARD DURING THIS TIME. LET YOUR POST-APOCALYPTIC MOTORING BEGIN ONCE THOSE UNPREPARED HAVE BEEN CLEARED FROM OUR ROADS'
LORD ROSE, CHAIRMAN,
THE POST-APOCALYPTIC MOTORING ASSOCIATION

Z-DAY

Z-Day is a nominal date zombie survivalists use to tag a particular date when the zombie hordes are in the ascendency. It's a concept used in planning. In reality, there won't be an official Z-Day. Things will start falling apart well before this date. Expect public transport to become sporadic and unreliable. Correction – expect public transport to become even more sporadic and unreliable. Think London night buses but with the added spice of zombies. As has been the case in previous emergencies, it's less to do with breakdowns and traffic but more to do with drivers and other support staff not turning up.

The first 48 hours of a real zombie outbreak emergency will be the most dangerous. If your mint-condition anti-zombie cruiser is sitting on the drive – this is likely the time it will be stolen, looted or destroyed beyond repair by desperate neighbours.

In reality, Z-Day will be a confusing period of weeks, a window when there is still a chance that the authorities will contain the outbreak. You won't be able to trust media reports so it's essential you have your own emergency protocols in place. For example, do you Bug-Out or go into lockdown at the first sign of 'cannibalism' in the street? This is a decision you will need to make as a zombie prepper and there are plenty of resources available online to support the development of your own warning system.

GETTING AROUND IN ZOMBIELAND

ASSESSING THE ZOMBIE CAPABILITIES

What about the dead themselves? Much of this manual is about preparing your transport options and plans for these end times so it's important you fully grasp the capabilities of these desperate and deadly creatures.

WHY FEAR THE WALKING DEAD?

A valid question asked by many new to zombie prepping. Many think that they might as well focus on their plans to battle bandits and human opponents, for example. However, although Zombies cannot use mass forms of transport, go for a Sunday drive or sign a hire-purchase agreement on a new Hyundai, they can get trapped under cars or buses, be swept along rivers with the current or wash up on beaches after drifting for weeks – in fact, they can 'travel' many hundreds, even thousands, of miles. This is something to take into account in your zombie preparedness planning, but what about 'normal' zombie walking? We know they are relentless but how far could zombies realistically walk?

Quick answer – we don't know. For example, if you bugged out in your pimped post-apocalyptic vehicle to the very north of Scotland, would the undead hordes of Glasgow, Manchester or even London eventually follow you?

What we do have is zombie scientist and walking dead egg-head Dr Raymond Carter's latest thinking on a biological model for zombie movement – a 500 page rip-roaring geek read. Here is the key message:

'WE DO NOT YET FULLY UNDERSTAND THE CHEMICAL REACTIONS TAKING PLACE WITHIN THOSE WITH THE ZOMBIC CONDITION BUT WE CAN ASSUME THAT A STANDARD ENERGY EQUATION IS AT WORK. THUS, ZOMBIES DO HAVE A FINITE ENERGY RESOURCE WHICH EXPLAINS WHY MANY CREATURES SIMPLY FALL INTO DORMANT STATES WHEN NOT AROUSED BY THE PROSPECT OF LIVING HUMAN MEAT'
DR RAYMOND CARTER

GETTING AROUND IN ZOMBIELAND
FACTS ABOUT ZOMBIES

▶ Zombies are real. They are scientific fact, with hundreds of sightings around the world and a dedicated (if under-funded) ministry within the UK government. There are pages of information on the Internet about the relatively new science of Zombiology. In particular, check out any work by Dr Kaleed Ahmed.

▶ The so-called 'zombic condition' is caused by a complex RNA virus, typically spread by bite or other fluid exchange. There is nothing supernatural about this very real threat to humanity. Most zombiologists (yeah, that's a word) are waiting for that term 'the big one' – that is a significant outbreak which overwhelms countries, even the world.

▶ Once infected, a human will typically transform into a zombie within 24 hours after exhibiting a series of flu-like symptoms. Once 'turned', zombies are slow and unbalanced with a vacant gaze and pallid, almost blue complexion. You cannot cure a zombie.

▶ Zombies hunger for human flesh and are relentless in their single-minded quest to feast on the living. They are no great thinkers but with their jagged finger nails, broken teeth and, above all their numbers, they are a very dangerous opponent.

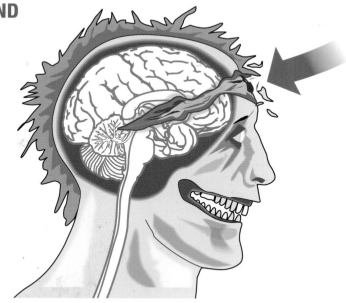

HOW TO KILL A ZOMBIE
Remember, the walking dead are not supernatural beings, they are not the undead. You can kill a zombie by destroying at least 80% of its brain function. Put another way – bash 'em hard in the head with something big and they will be stopped.

▶ ZOMBIE CAPABILITIES

It's vital that you understand the physical capabilities of the walking dead. There are different forms of zombies but, as a rule, they cannot run, use ladders, hire bikes or jet off for sneaky weekends in Prague. Slow, pondering and remorseless – that's them.

ZOMBIE ENERGY

Zombies conserve energy by entering a catatonic state. Little is known about the digestive process of the walking dead. No researcher has really fancied taking the job on.

ZOMBIE SPEED

A whole body zombie will typically amble along at a below average walking pace. They are capable of bursts of greater speed if motivated by the prospect of human meat.

ZOMBIE AGILITY

Zombies do not feel pain so the loss of a foot or whole limb does not prevent movement. Unstable at the best of times, however, zombies with missing body parts will be reduced to moving at a snail's pace, sometimes even reduced to crawling along the ground like a putrid worm.

ZOMBIE BRAINPOWER

The walking dead aren't going to win any pub quizzes but they have the brain capacity to engage arms and legs to drive movement. They are capable of basic shambling but actions such as jumping can cause issues.

ZOMBIE SENSES

Our best research indicates that humans become chronically short-sighted after infection. Zombies therefore have poor eye sight at a distance. Their sense of touch is also diminished. However, they seem to develop a keen sense of smell, particularly for the scent of living human flesh.

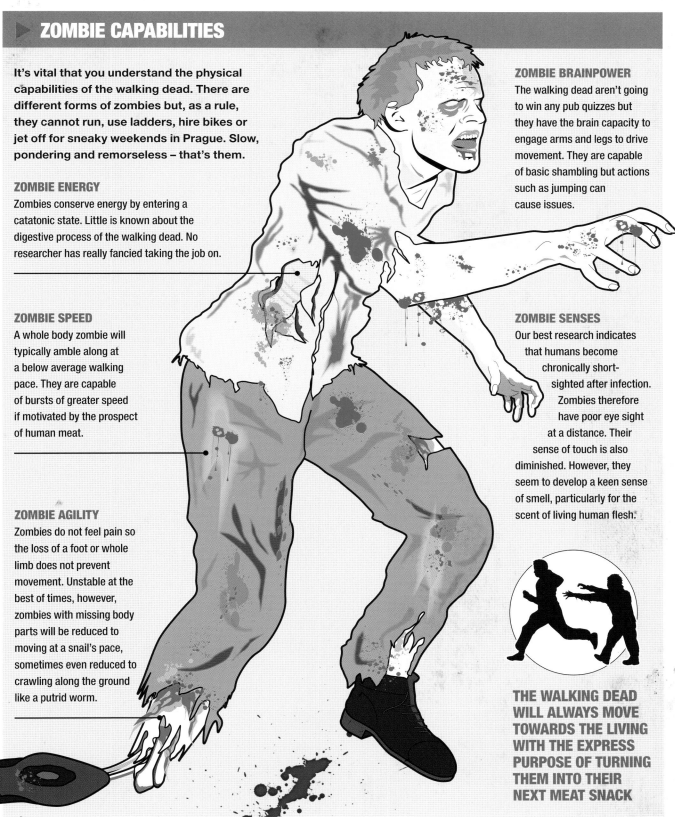

THE WALKING DEAD WILL ALWAYS MOVE TOWARDS THE LIVING WITH THE EXPRESS PURPOSE OF TURNING THEM INTO THEIR NEXT MEAT SNACK

11

GETTING AROUND IN ZOMBIELAND

ZOMBIE SPEED TEST

In August 2016, the Ministry of Zombies teamed up with the Royal Jordanian Broadcasting Corporation (RJBC) to make a unique documentary which, working under scientific instruction, sought to examine the different performance capabilities of the main types of zombie – a vital factor when considering transport issues in the aftermath of a zombie apocalypse.

A number of zombie specimens were obtained, categorised and then assessed in a series of physical tests jokingly referred to by the film crew as the 'Zombie Olympics'. Over a period of several weeks, the study sought to establish performance credentials for the various types of zombie. Crucially, this information could help survivalists answer the age old question – do zombies shamble like in the George A. Romero films or race like sprint runners as in *28 Days Later*.

There is no official test evidence on kiddie ghouls as awkward World Health Organisation (WHO) legal restrictions prevent testing but most preppers swear that they are faster than regular zombies and more dextrous.

0–1 MPH
CRAWLERS
(SCRAPPERS, SNAKIES, DRAGGERS)

Typically, crawlers are missing their legs or the entire bottom section of the body. Technically speaking, crawlers could be dragging remaining body parts such as legs dangling on a tendon or stray intestines.

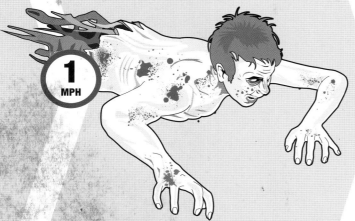

1 MPH

CAPABILITIES
These desperate creatures move by crawling along at a very slow pace with a top speed of much less than 1 mph. Crawlers are more dangerous as they can easily be missed, particularly in grass land. They are adept at crawling through any low open windows or even unprotected ventilation ducts. Do not underestimate these creatures.

2–3 MPH
FRESH OR CLASSIC
(NOOBS, NEWBIES, MUNCHIES)

A classic blue-grey skin coloured zombie will be the most common type of ghoul.

3 MPH

CAPABILITIES
Slow, lumbering but is capable of staggering towards the living. Top speed is 2–3 mph. Most of the time, these creatures mill around aimlessly then rest in a dormant state until alerted by noise or scent.

GETTING AROUND IN ZOMBIELAND
BEWARE OF SEVERED HEADS

Zombie heads can survive for weeks when severed from the infected body and are a surprisingly dangerous form of the walking dead. Severed heads are particularly common in the early weeks of the apocalypse as amateur zombie bashers often believe that decapitation alone will 'kill' a zombie.

Severed heads are basically snapping jaws and so can only move through this action. They are therefore capable of rolling slowly towards a target but in most cases they are unable to move more than a metre. Instead, they tend to 'sit' and wait for victims.

3–4 MPH
LIMBLESS WONDERS
(DUMMIES, BIRDIES)

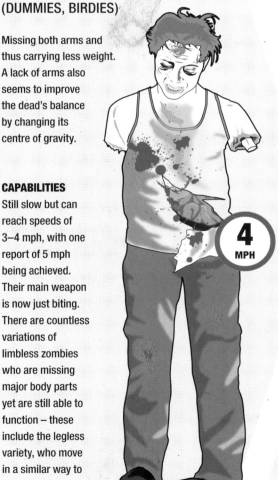

Missing both arms and thus carrying less weight. A lack of arms also seems to improve the dead's balance by changing its centre of gravity.

CAPABILITIES
Still slow but can reach speeds of 3–4 mph, with one report of 5 mph being achieved. Their main weapon is now just biting. There are countless variations of limbless zombies who are missing major body parts yet are still able to function – these include the legless variety, who move in a similar way to crawlers.

4+ MPH
INFECTED HUMAN
(DEADS, VIROS)

Humans infected with the zombic virus are likely to be panicky and desperate. Some will display bite marks, others no sign at all of infection.

CAPABILITIES
Enhanced human abilities, fuelled by an adrenalin rich surge caused by their recent infection. Psychological studies have shown that, despite their knowledge of infection, infected humans will move into a denial stage in which they may convince themselves that they are somehow immune or uninfected. During this time, they will be capable of any crime to keep their infection a secret, including murder.

GETTING AROUND IN ZOMBIELAND

THE RIGHT VEHICLE FOR YOU

There are many factors to consider when deciding on your choice of vehicle for the zombie apocalypse. It is advised that you use this volume like a workbook – keep a note pad handy and write down the factors critical to your plans. Read the case studies through and look at the plans before deciding on the right transport mix or vehicle for you. Remember that many preppers will keep a range of vehicles – something light for foraging in the immediate area and a more serious vehicle for bugging out.

ESSENTIAL FEATURES

Inexperienced zombie preppers often skip any detailed analysis and move right on to selecting the vehicle they think will 'do the job' during a zombie outbreak. Indeed, there are Internet forums filled with debates about on-road versus off-road capability, whether new sports utility vehicles can really do the job and if adapting a heavy goods vehicle to create the ultimate fighting platform could really work. There are hundreds of options out there from your old Honda Civic with some barbed wire wrapped around it to a fully equipped gyrocopter.

Whatever vehicle or vehicles you select, here's a checklist of important features. Obviously, if it's just an off-road scrambler you intend to use for foraging then you won't need all this kit but for any longer-distance travel, start here then take out elements if they're not required. You'll come across countless guides and top 10 lists as you develop your skills as a survivalist. Use this information and any others you find as source material and adapt according to your own needs.

- ► On-board Bug-Out Bag
- ► Drinking water for at least 48 hours
- ► Emergency rations for at least 48 hours
- ► Clubbing weapons such as wrenches or cricket bats
- ► Any firearms you can get your hands on
- ► Sleeping bags and blankets
- ► Survival tool box with spare vehicle parts
- ► Emergency first aid kit
- ► Jerry cans of fuel
- ► A selection of maps
- ► Winch and ropes if you have the space
- ► A few spare tins of food for bartering

1. TIME

A very practical consideration. No one knows when the zombies will strike. It is most likely to be in the next 10 years but no one knows for sure. So, you need to be able to commit the time and resources to maintaining your vehicles, including training and all of the other associated costs.

2. BUDGET

A major limiting factor for most. You'll find options easily costing £100,000 in this book but this kind of expense just won't be feasible for everyone. The good news is you don't need to spend big but you do need to spend wisely. For example, it may be cost effective to select one of the conversion kits outlined later and fit it to your current car when the dead rise.

3. THE PLAN

Staying put or Bugging-Out? It's pointless investing in a fully apocalypse-ready recreational vehicle if you intend to fortify your home and then only later venture out into your local area. Consider your options carefully – you can assess your transport needs once you have a strategy.

8. MAINTENANCE

Something which has become more relevant in recent years with the computerisation of many modern cars. Some preppers deliberately pick pre-1980s vehicles because they can be maintained with non-specialist tools. Others tear out the unnecessary tech components on their vehicles hoping to make them easy to maintain and resistant to features of the apocalypse such as electromagnetic pulses (EMPs).

7. FUEL

There's a serious choice to be made here. You'll find a whole section on fuel types in this book but it's a subject on which few zombie preppers agree. Petrol, diesel or alternative – it's a personal choice – each have their advantages and disadvantages. You should consider fuel storage and access to further supplies.

CHOOSING THE VEHICLE OR VEHICLES YOU WANT TO FACE THE END OF THE WORLD IN IS ONE OF THE BIGGEST DECISIONS YOU'LL EVER MAKE AS A ZOMBIE PREPPER

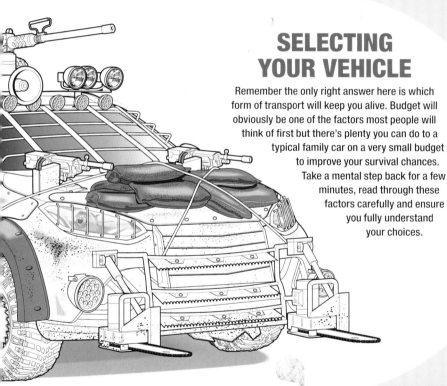

SELECTING YOUR VEHICLE

Remember the only right answer here is which form of transport will keep you alive. Budget will obviously be one of the factors most people will think of first but there's plenty you can do to a typical family car on a very small budget to improve your survival chances. Take a mental step back for a few minutes, read through these factors carefully and ensure you fully understand your choices.

6. LOCATION

Exactly where do you call home? If you live on an isolated farm then you have a good chance of keeping an apocalypse gyrocopter under wraps and secure until it's needed. If you live in the city centre, you're likely to need a robust road warrior to battle the inevitable rise of the street gangs. Also, think about where you are going to store your vehicle.

4. SIZE OF GROUP

Are you flying solo or do you have a family to consider? Exactly who will be using your Bug-Out Vehicles? You may need several if you plan to travel as a group or in convoy. Some preppers prefer to invest in a group of vehicles to ensure that they're not left stranded. But others insist Bug-Out Vehicles like converted coaches will be unstoppable in the wasteland, operating like powerful tanks to crush the zombies.

5. BLEND IN

Consider going for a 'basic' model to blend into the apocalyptic background – great for either looting or bugging out over a serious distance. Or, would you prefer to display your post-apoc credentials and weapons with pride, to deter any would-be attackers?

REMEMBER

Keep your working plans confidential. In any conversations with mechanics or garages you can always say you're considering taking up banger racing.

BASIC TRANSPORT

Here in the UK and Europe, there aren't many car showrooms demonstrating the latest Mad Max style road warrior vehicle. As a continent we are poorly prepared in terms of transport requirements. So, let's start at the beginning.

This book is not a zombie survival manual for beginners. We are going to assume that if you have read this far, you're already aware of the importance of keeping fit and active as you prepare for the inevitable zombie apocalypse. So, you should already be familiar with an established fitness regime which includes walking or trekking practice. Regardless of whether you face the apocalypse with a fully pimped apocalyptic tank or an old Nissan Micra with a few pieces of barbed wire nailed on, there will be times when your primary form of transport is by foot. Remember to try to get at least a 6–8 mile training walk in every week as part of your training regime.

▶ This section will look at a number of 'unpowered' transport options including animals and cycles – two methods often mentioned on zombie prepper forums.
▶ Don't forget that there are other options to support you if you are on foot such as various handcarts – although if you do plan to travel the wasteland with a pimped Tesco shopping trolley as your vehicle of choice then this probably isn't the book for you.
▶ Easily available before the dead rise and after Z-Day, you can simply check out any DIY store to get yourself a cart.
▶ Even if it's not your primary form of transport, it is worth grabbing one and keeping it in the boot of your main vehicle.

OPTION 1
HANDCARTS

Not really a 'form of transport' but if you are planning to travel a short distance to, for example, an improved location, survival experts swear by this kind of vehicle. Human-powered, they make surprisingly light work of your supplies should you need to relocate. Not ideal if you are in a hurry but easy enough to just drop should you need to if any zombies shamble too close for comfort. Industrial jumbo hand-wagons can handle loads up to 630 kg – that's a lot of Bug-Out Gear but realistically your range will be limited to a few hundred metres. Easily available before the dead rise and after, you can simply check out any DIY store and help yourself to a cart.

 Handy for moving supplies and looting but, come on, is this really how you imagined the end of the world to be? Is this really the form of transport you wanted to end up with?

OPTION 2
SACK TRUCKS

Similar to handcarts, these can be found in most factories and warehouses. Again, survival experts make good use of these kinds of tools for moving kit around. You won't exactly look like Mad Max dashing between Bug-Out locations with a sack truck stacked with boxes but consider that if you do your back in lifting a heavy load in normal life, for sure it's painful but not a huge issue with access to medical and healthcare resources, but if you do yourself a serious injury in zombie-country then you could end up a very cheap meat snack. A quality handcart or sack truck will enable you to safely move far more Bug-Out supplies than say a back-pack.

 Again, not the best option if you are going for that cool, road warrior type vibe but maybe the supplies you forage will keep you and your anorak alive.

OPTION 3
ADULT SCOOTERS

Seen in every park and playground across the country, scooters also come in robust adult versions. In particular, 'Dirt Scooters' are very different beasts from your typical pink-tasselled Anna and Elsa Pink Magic Scooter. These machines are built with serious off-road conditions in mind and for around £400, you get rugged over-sized pneumatic tyres, beefy chrome handlebars and a hardened steel tube frame. Made for stunt riders, these scooters are ideal for short-range foraging trips and are tough enough to see you through an apocalypse. Add a stylish canvas front-bag and scary warning horn to provide your scooter with a more 'end of the world' feel.

 A useful option and can cover some good distances but a high centre of gravity makes them vulnerable. Plus, you'll look a bit of a tool scooting through the wasteland.

BASIC TRANSPORT
KNOW YOUR LIMITS

The UK's Health and Safety Executive estimates that over 30,000 people are seriously injured in bicycle related accidents every year and a further 14,000 in skateboard or scooter incidents. A startling 391 people were killed in Sack Truck Accidents (STAs) across the country in 2016 alone. If you are opting for any form of transport which relies on you to power it, remember to be fully aware of how to safely operate and maintain your 'vehicle'. Your own physical fitness will also be an important factor. Overloading your handcart or running out of puff as you cycle uphill could easily get you munched in a zombie-ridden wasteland.

SKATEBOARDS ARE UNSTABLE, UNPREDICTABLE AND PRONE TO GOING OUT OF CONTROL — THOSE NEW TO SKATEBOARDS WILL NOT SURVIVE LONG IN THE WASTELANDS

OPTION 4
SKATEBOARDS

There are some serious skateboard models out there which can enable you to travel serious distances at a good pace. However, there are two serious survival issues with skateboards. Firstly, whereas a scooter can be mastered in a few days, a skateboard takes substantially longer and it's much easier to have an accident if you don't know what you are doing. Secondly, many skateboards have toughened plastic wheels which make enough noise to draw in any zombie in the vicinity. If you're an expert, you'll be travelling fast enough to dodge them. If not, you could end up with a trail of dead followers, just waiting for you to trip up on the nearest kerb.

 Skateboards are hard to master and it's far too easy to have a serious fall. Add to this the fact that most skateboards are noisy enough to attract every zombie in a mile radius.

OPTION 5
ROLLER BLADES

From 1970s-style disco roller skates to modern high-tech in-line skates, there is no shortage of options for when you want to attach small wheels to your feet and speed your way out of trouble. And, with experienced skaters hitting average speeds of up to 15 mph, roller blades might be the solution to outrunning the dead and even bandits. But, it's not for the amateur. Roller skating is one of those things — easy to try — hard to master. It is recommended that you get at least 8 hours practice skating in per week if you plan to use any form of skates as your post-apocalyptic transport. Also, don't forget to practice carrying your full Bug-Out Kit.

 Practice makes perfect with any form of roller skates so if you plan to use them to escape the zombies, better get out there now and start to boogie.

OPTION 6
CYCLING

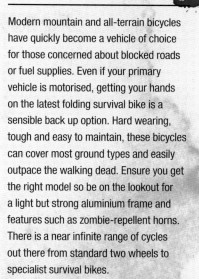

Modern mountain and all-terrain bicycles have quickly become a vehicle of choice for those concerned about blocked roads or fuel supplies. Even if your primary vehicle is motorised, getting your hands on the latest folding survival bike is a sensible back up option. Hard wearing, tough and easy to maintain, these bicycles can cover most ground types and easily outpace the walking dead. Ensure you get the right model so be on the lookout for a light but strong aluminium frame and features such as zombie-repellent horns. There is a near infinite range of cycles out there from standard two wheels to specialist survival bikes.

 The right choice of survival bicycle will see you through the zombie apocalypse in style but get plenty of fitness training in before the dead rise.

BASIC TRANSPORT

BIKES AND CYCLING

Cycling will be a very practical way to get around once civilisation collapses. Cycles are found everywhere, are easy to maintain and with storage panniers attached there can be room for some foraged booty. Choosing wisely will be all important or you could end up battling a group of desperate survivors on a pink Halfords Twinkle. Cycling is well covered on zombie survival forums and most topics focus on mountain or all-terrain bikes which have robust frames and useful gearing. Equally important is personal fitness – a factor often over-looked.

For a reasonable cost, it's possible to kit an entire family out with specially built Bug-Out Survival Bicycles such as the Z-Navigator Folding Bikes (PZ-17) made by the very successful Flying Pigeon Bicycle Company in China. This all-terrain bike and its accompanying children's versions are possibly the best selling survival bicycles of all time. However, you can get some of the same benefits by adapting your own bike, as long as you start with a robust model and consider zombie-gunk proofing the gears and brakes.

▶ INDIAN ARMY HAVILDAR QUADCYCLE

The army of the Republic of India is one of the largest organisations in the world, with well over 1.3 million soldiers and support staff in service at any one time. It has been widely respected around the world for its prowess in emergency planning since a commission was set up in 2010 to look at how the nation should prepare for a major viral outbreak, and it's no surprise that the planning team immediately turned to the power of the bicycle, or more accurately, the quadcycle. The challenge was simple but on an enormous scale. With over a billion people living in a vast country, how could the armed services maintain law and order in the chaotic environment of a zombie outbreak? With nothing suitable available on the open market, they turned to Indian manufacturer Tata Steel to create a unique post-apocalyptic vehicle.

'THE HAVILDAR QUADCYCLE IS CHEAP TO BUILD AND EASY TO MAINTAIN. A THREE MAN RELIEF TEAM CAN TRAVEL SAFELY FOR HUNDREDS OF MILES ACROSS ZOMBIE-INFESTED TERRITORY'
COLONEL 'SPOKES' SHARMA

INDIAN ARMY HAVILDAR QUADCYCLE (LIGHT SURVIVAL VEHICLE 713TC)
Indian Armed Forces, Republic of India

LOCATION
Plans held in the Bursar's Office, Rashtriya Indian Military College, Dehradun

PURPOSE
A dependable light transport vehicle, designed for human-powered patrol and reconnaissance duty. Unofficially, it is believed this vehicle is at the heart of the Republic of India's national zombie survival plan.

TECHNICAL SPECIFICATIONS
Gusseted, reinforced steel frame, aluminium alloy floorboard and panels. Steel component front zombie guards, chain-guards and brake arms. 10-speed gearing system. Base model weight 106 kg, Indian Army Havildar estimated weight 150 kg. Length 190 cm, width 125 cm, height 182 cm.

ARMAMENTS
Standard configuration with options to add any weapons carried by the riders – two Glock 17 semi-automatic pistols, fittings for an IMI Negev light machine gun, plus an AK-47Z on the back shelf.

RANGE
400 miles with basic maintenance. Service every 500 miles depending on usage.

CREW
2–4 with kit. 3 in survival configuration with one sleeping zone in the rear.

BUDGET
The Indian Army forces have declined to answer this question. A standard base model quadcycle from a quality Italian manufacturer will cost around £6,000. Extras to bring it up to the specification of the Indian Army Havildar Quadcycle could cost as much as £10,000.

USAGE GUIDELINES
Colonel 'Spokes' Sharma – 'Indian military forces currently have 10 Havildar Quadcycle deployed, with a further 200 being built. All 10 vehicles are with the Sikh Regiment and are under trial. We firmly believe that in a post-apocalyptic scenario, being able to move troops and supplies quickly and without a reliance on either fuel or electronic subsystems, will enable us to maintain law and order and provide relief. I believe it's no exaggeration to say that this vehicle could save the Republic by stemming the tide of the walking dead.'

FEATURES

▶ Stainless steel
reinforced fenders and
panelled cage to protect a 3 person
crew, including frontal ram bars

▶ Mottled green Indian Army patented
anti-viral paint, with chemical zombie
blood resistance

▶ Tension Perspex window shields, which can
be lowered to seal the vehicle if required

▶ Directional LED head, tail and search lights for
emergency rescue missions

▶ Integrated 10-gear sealed drive system,
based on 2 active peddlers and 1
slave pedal unit

▶ Aluminium alloy floorboard and tubular body,
offering a robust anti-roll unit

▶ Four wheel drum brakes with anti-zombie
gunk seals

▶ Ultimate Tata-K 'mag' wheels with
strengthened Vishna brand tyres

▶ Forward mounting for light
machine gun, with ammunition
box feed storage just below

▶ Quad solar panels supplying power
to a control array on the front control
panel. The controller can direct power
to lights and a military-grade satellite
navigation system

▶ Secure roof storage area for soldiers' kit.
Standard emergency Bug-Out Supplies
include food, water and a purification unit
to supply 4 people for up to a week.

TRIALS REPORT

In January 2017, a 3-man crew from 4th
Battalion Sikh Regiment took a Havildar
Quadcycle on a 400 mile journey, maintaining
a constantly moving vehicle over the
complete 6 day journey. The crew rode
in 4-hour shifts, using a 2-seat survival
configuration, with a sleeping space behind.
The vehicle averaged a steady 3 mph and
was in continuous use. The men ate and
slept on board the quadcycle.

BASIC TRANSPORT

BMX RAIDING

Zombie preppers rarely consider a full-sized BMX when making their Bug-Out plans but these robust off-road and trick bikes have much about them to recommend, particularly if used in groups for raiding or foraging purposes. BMXs come in several model types – ideally, you'd be looking for a quality 'dirt style' bike which has tyres with a deeper tread for better off-road manoeuvrability. Good jumping ability, robust build quality and a very tight turning circle make BMXs suitable for all sorts of urban activity and models such as the Shimano Apocalypse X even provide a little storage in specially designed mini panniers. BMXs such as the Shimano Apocalypse range cost in excess of £1,000 per bike but a decent model can be picked up for a fraction of the price. It is worth checking online to study the BMX raiding techniques of gangs such as the London-based Krucial Krew, who operated in the mid-1990s pioneering BMX combat techniques such as the 'hop out of danger', 'death wheelie' and 'rotter slap'.

BASIC TRANSPORT
APOCALYPSE CYCLING

In March 2017, *Survivalist Monthly* asked its over 8,000 readers which form of bicycle would be their ideal choice for an apocalypse. No reference was made to zombies but the results still confirmed that most preppers opt for a 'do it yourself' adapted mountain bike as opposed to a purpose built bike such as the Z-Navigator PZ-17 or any other model type.

3%   **ELECTRIC-ASSIST BIKE**
'Economical and quiet, these bikes will gently motor you out of trouble'

5%   **PURPOSE-BUILT APOCALYPSE MOUNTAIN BIKE**
'This is the only model I'd go for, something with a good range in case my main vehicle breaks down'

8%   **BMX OR SIMILAR**
'I plan to stay in an urban environment so I need something cheap and robust'

13%   **FOLDING BIKE**
'It's certainly not stylish but it fits in the back of my Bug-Out Vehicle and provides another transport option if needed'

71%   **A STANDARD MOUNTAIN/ ALL-TERRAIN BIKE**
'Pimped with my own added adaptations'

SURVEY FROM *SURVIVALIST MONTHLY*, MARCH/APRIL 2017 – 2,167 RESPONDENTS

THE CASSIDY APOCALYPSE SHOPPING TROLLEY

In late 2015, the Ministry of Zombies sponsored a series of zombie combat workshops for the elderly entitled 'Senior Citizen, Senior Survivor'. They taught the fundamentals of zombie combat including how to use accessories such as walking sticks and zimmer frames to deal with the walking dead. At the Belfast session, one 81-year-old grandmother shocked the trainers by turning up with a loaded antique blunderbuss gun. Mrs Eileen Cassidy went on not only to demonstrate her black belt in karate but showed designs from her own range of survival wheeled shopping trolleys known as 'Cassidy Carts'.

USAGE GUIDELINES

The shopping trolley is dual purpose and can be used to either transport supplies such as tea and biscuits or, once a small seat is added, be used to ferry babies and toddlers around. 'The first change we made to the basic "Budget Model" trolley was to fix those bloody wheels,' reports Mrs Cassidy. 'No more wayward steering. These trolleys stay on course. A nice man from BAE Weapons Systems helped me fit some front rocket launchers and fine-tuned my designs for a street-legal multi-flare gun. This trolley will see you through the apocalypse whether you are foraging for supplies at your local supermarket, battling the zombies or dealing with some bad guys – you'll be prepared.'

'WE DO NOT APPROVE OR SANCTION ANY OF MRS CASSIDY'S ADAPTATIONS TO OUR STANDARD TROLLEY DESIGN. HER TROLLEY IS A MENACE AND DOWNRIGHT DANGEROUS IN THE WRONG HANDS'
MICHELLE LEWIS, TROLLEY SOLUTIONS DIRECTOR, TROLLEY SOLUTIONS LTD

FEATURES

- Titanium steel alloy frame with a secret ingredient added by Mrs Cassidy before assembly (scone crumbs)
- Generous Bug-Out Storage Pouch for up to 72 hours of supplies
- In-built camelback water pouch plus purification unit
- Thermal tea cup holder
- Hobnob or Rich Tea pouch
- Waterproof scratch card pouch
- Available in black or mottled combat camouflage
- Four wheel assembly – all can turn 360 degrees for agility
- Spiked rear wheels enable users to deploy a 'high flick' sending the cart into any approaching zombie
- Shotgun pouch
- Clubbing weapon holder
- Emergency sheet converts the cart into a temporary shelter
- Triple stun grenade holder
- Emergency smoke deployment unit, trigger is located on the handle

Since 2015, Mrs Cassidy has been just as busy and has recently been working with famous children's buggy empire McLaren to create a pilot 'Apocalypse Shopping Trolley'. These trolleys will come equipped with enough firepower to take on the zombie horde but also a range of educational toys to distract your toddler as you battle through the smoking wasteland. Mrs Cassidy has been working with her daughter-in-law Lauren on this project but things have been slow as Lauren is currently getting an extension to her house. 'It'll be nice for the summer,' reports Mrs Cassidy, 'but I really think she could have planned the building work more carefully.'

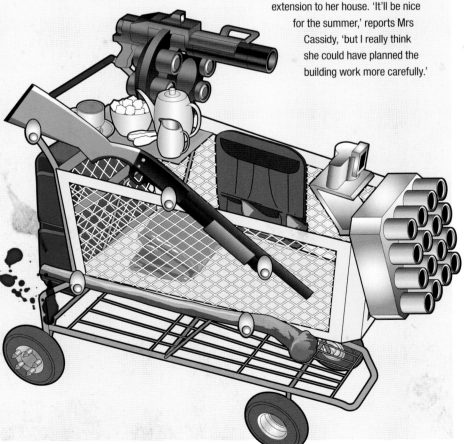

BASIC TRANSPORT

COPING WITH DISABILITIES

The Ministry of Zombies has worked for many years with disability charities and other organisations to support the very active debate around how those with disabilities can survive a zombie apocalypse. Up to 2010, much of this work was academic and followed UN guidelines in areas such as using a white sheet to call for assistance and waiting for help to arrive. A meeting with Captain Steve 'Rusty' Langdon in 2011 changed everything. This 35-year-old US Gulf War veteran was the first to create a purpose built zombie-fighting wheelchair and has continued his work, developing a fully integrated survival scooter. But, before we get into the mechanics, it's worth considering Rusty's three key pointers.

▶ **GET INTO THE RIGHT MIND-SET FROM THE START**
The zombies don't care if you have a disability. You have to rely on yourself and any trusted friends. Get educated. Get trained. And, get prepared.

▶ **CONSIDER CAREFULLY YOUR OWN NEEDS**
Think long-term. Stock up on any medication you need. Select the right mode of transport for your situation. I'm unable to use my legs so the Zomb-Chair is ideal.

▶ **ON Z-DAY, EVERYTHING CHANGES**
Sure you'll still have a disability but with your training and a bit of luck, you'll also be a survivor, just like all the other survivors. Use your skills to team up with others – don't be a victim and be prepared to fight to survive.

▶ THE STANNA WASTELAND SURVIVAL SCOOTER

The Stanna Wasteland Survival Scooter is a next-generation personal mobility solution for the zombie apocalypse. It features a powerful battery-powered engine and a host of anti-zombie features, as well as being an impressive wasteland cruiser. Developed by Gulf War veteran and Disability Survival Champion Steve 'Rusty' Langdon and Stanna Mobility Solutions, it was built to cope with anything the end of the world can throw at you. 'A few years ago, I was part of the team that created the Zomb-Chair. I took a bit of flak as it was considered pretty expensive so teamed up with a commercial manufacturer and together we cooked something up which might just rock your world.'

'HAVING A DISABILITY DOESN'T HAVE TO MAKE YOU A TARGET. THERE ARE PLENTY OF ABLE-BODIED PEOPLE OUT THERE WHO ARE POORLY-EDUCATED AND ILL-PREPARED FOR THE ZOMBIES'
STEVE 'RUSTY' LANGDON

THE STANNA WASTELAND SURVIVAL SCOOTER
Patent holder: Steve Langdon, Arizona. Licensee Stanna Mobility Solutions

PURPOSE
Short-range post-apocalyptic personal transporter

TECHNICAL SPECIFICATIONS
Overall height 137 cm, width 75 cm, length 160 cm. Maximum gradient 10 degrees, driven by 4 x 75 Ah Supa-Z Sealed Apocalypse batteries. Ground clearance 8 cm. Includes dashboard LCD display, reporting on the 22 zombie-movement detecting sensors set around the vehicle.

ARMAMENTS
None as standard but plenty of upgrade options including rear-shooting nail-gun, M16 fixing point, shotgun pouch and arm-rest bolt gun. Most of the customers to date are happy to manage their own weapons configuration. Anything supplied directly from Stanna must meet the legal requirements for the country it is being imported into.

RANGE
A typical mobility scooter will manage around 10 miles at a steady speed of 4 mph but the Stanna Wasteland Survival Scooter has quadrupled the power of a standard model and in tests has comfortably managed 100 miles, with a cruising speed of 5–6 mph. It has a top speed of 10 mph, more than enough to outrun any zombies. There are plans for a larger petrol-engine model from mid-2018 onwards.

CREW
1 plus Bug-Out Bag and support goods. Will run with another person if required but range is reduced.

BUDGET
For a standard base model, built to order, £5,000 plus delivery. A Motability grant may be available in England and Wales. In Scotland and Northern Ireland, users may be entitled to a free unit via their NHS Disability Zombie Awareness Scheme.

⚠ BASIC TRANSPORT
DISABILITIES

Many disabled zombie preppers go down the 'staying put' route, with a focus on home fortification and laying down stores at the expense of any transportation considerations. Vehicles such as the Wasteland Survival Scooter are changing this, with many preppers unwilling to sit waiting for a rescue which they know may never come. Disabled preppers have choices and there is a growing market in adapted survival vehicles, which is opening up all kinds of options.

> 'A WELL-TRAINED PERSON WITH A DISABILITY, WHO HAS PREPARED FOR A MAJOR ZOMBIE OUTBREAK, STANDS AN EXCELLENT CHANCE OF SURVIVING THE CHAOS'
> **STEVE 'RUSTY' LANGDON**

USAGE GUIDELINES

'The Stanna Wasteland Survival Scooter is the most powerful personal mobility scooter on the market and the only one specially built to cope with a zombie apocalypse and the unique challenges that emergency will bring for those with disabilities. It's tough, it's fast and it's powerful – it's a useful addition to anyone preparing for the wasteland. However, you have to see it as part of your Bug-Out System. This scooter will handle many of your transport needs but you still need to consider fortifying a home base. Think through your re-charging station and get your on-board weapons mix right. I'm a personal fan of a decent shotgun as at least part of your on-board arsenal.'

FEATURES

▶ Twin rear view mirrors for all-around rear-visibilty plus rear camera
▶ Anti-roll back system prevents scooter from rolling backwards on hills. Rear anti-tip wheels as standard prevent the dead pushing the scooter over during an attack.

▶ Freewheel facility allows user to roll-down hills as required
▶ Full cross-body seat-belt
▶ 22 motion sensors set around the vehicle, calibrated to detect both human and zombie movement.
▶ Detachable Sensor pickets – stick sensors in ground set perimeter defence
▶ Solar charged battery
▶ Armoured 360 degree swivel chair
▶ Rear anti-tip wheels for extra stability
▶ Automatic electromagnetic braking system
▶ Rear-firing bolt gun – like a nail gun – spread can be set and fires at different levels.

▶ Jacked suspension offering 8 cm ground-clearance, for off-roading
▶ Waterproof up to 1 metre
▶ Virtually silent battery powered motors
▶ Can be dismantled in a few minutes – manufactured in 5 main pieces
▶ Puncture proof tyres
▶ All-weather protective camouflage scooter cape
▶ Survival saddle bags
▶ Front Combat Basket, with weapons storage option
▶ Distraction flares – a set of triple flares on each side.

POST-APOCALYPTIC INVENTIONS

How to get around after a major zombie outbreak is not a new concern for zombie survivalists. Indeed the earliest documentary evidence is from Lady Nora Brightlings's article 'Velopeds and Escaping the Blight', published in *Punch* Magazine in 1883 – in it she considers new-fangled free-wheeling bicycles terrifying in London parks but '...a most ideal route from which to flee the recently risen.' However, whilst much progress has been made since this time, the road is paved with some of the most stupid and pointless zombie survival travel contraptions. The most ineffective, useless and in most cases downright dangerous transport options ever. Some of these products are still available, particularly via disreputable online traders.

▶ ANTI-BLIGHT ARMOUR

Sir Richard Splashworth took a standard suit of expensive armour and reinforced all of the joints with toughened leather to create one of the first zombie survival suits. He confidently predicted that a knight wearing his armour could continue to travel the land, rescuing those in need. Noble idea.

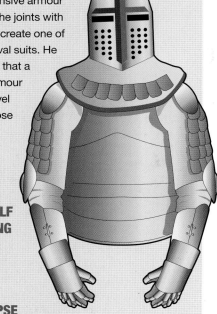

SIR RICHARD SPLASHWORTH HAS SECURED A PLACE FOR HIMSELF IN ZOMBIE FIGHTING HISTORY AS THE CREATOR OF THE WORST OUTFIT IN WHICH TO FACE A ZOMBIE APOCALYPSE

Unfortunately, there were several problems. Firstly, the suit weighed over 20 kg and you needed to be a superman to move in it. Secondly, those wearing it were so slow that they could be quickly over-taken and over-powered by the ravenous hordes. But worst of all, the foolish Sir Splashworth ordered that the leather joints be greased with pork fat, which it turned out the dead find particularly tasty.

In summary, it's so heavy you can hardly move, any rain and it rusts, and the zombies just love munching on those pork fat-soaked leather joints. Thanks for nothing Sir Splashworth – avoid this and any modern variations.

▶ GARIBALDI SPRING-SHOES

Advertised in the 1920s as the cheapest way to escape ghouls, inventor Pascal Garibaldi created this apocalypse footwear after seeing a well-known circus act performing with similar mechanisms attached to their feet.

After a few unsuccessful attempts, Garibaldi finally secured a patent on his creation in 1925 and the Garibaldi Spring-shoes were demonstrated at the 1926 World Fair in Philadelphia by famous strongman Fabian McDuff. According to contemporary sources, the giant Scotsman entered a fenced off area with no less than 4 zombies and no weapon. The strongman successfully evaded the ghouls, effortlessly springing over 10 metres in the air and from corner to corner. As an interesting side note, his kilted attire caused something of scandal due to his energetic leaping and is rumoured to have caused several female on-lookers to faint.

However, consumer test documents from the time report that the shoes were 'uncontrollable', sending the wearer in any direction and at heights of up to 15 metres in the air.

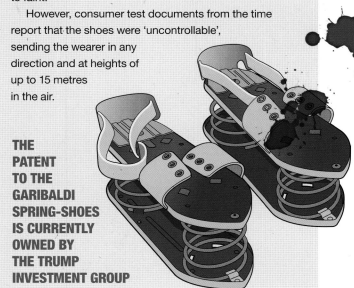

THE PATENT TO THE GARIBALDI SPRING-SHOES IS CURRENTLY OWNED BY THE TRUMP INVESTMENT GROUP

THE SINCLARE C5Z

Underpowered, with the driver low enough to be within easy grabbing distance of the nearest zombie – even the legless crawling kind – the Sinclare C5z is possibly the worst form of post-apocalyptic transport known to man. To cap all of that, it was sold at the time for a pocket-busting price of almost £3,000 – remember, you could buy a lot of Duran Duran records in 1985 for that price.

Birmingham-based inventor Roger Sutcliffe took a basic Sinclair C5 model, added a 2 metre whip aerial (there is no radio included on the vehicle) and crudely attempted to boost the battery power. The result was a vehicle ill-suited to any post-apocalyptic travel. He also attempted to fool willing buyers by advertising the hopeless vehicle as an official 'Sinclare' model, hoping to trade on the early success of Clive Sinclair's C5.

Everything was wrong on the C5z. It was open, slow as a zombie and emitted a low hum which attracted every zombie from miles around. Plus, you look like a right wally driving it. No storage space and a battery guaranteed to leave you stranded. To add insult to injury, models can still be bought online and so the madness of the C5z continues to this day. Beat that world.

THIS DISASTROUS ZOMBIE SURVIVAL VEHICLE IS NOW PERMANENTLY OFF THE ROAD AFTER A SUCCESSFUL LEGAL CASE WAS BROUGHT BY SIR CLIVE SINCLAIR. THANK YOU SIR CLIVE!

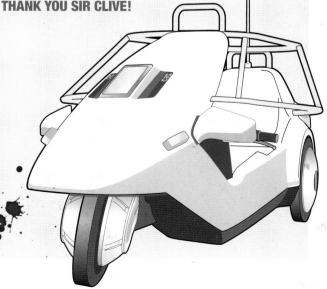

SILICON VALLEY SURVIVAL EGG

Designed by some of the smartest beards in Silicon valley, the Survival Egg is $430,000 worth of stick your head in the sand snowflake generation thinking at its best. It's meant to keep the occupant safe in any disaster, from zombies to global warming. A secure high-technology mobile cocoon, with more entertainment options than most homes and even a soothing voice which can be turned on to re-assure the occupant that everything is going to be OK.

THE SURVIVAL EGG IS THE PRODUCT OF MUDDLED THINKING BY SERIOUSLY INTELLIGENT PEOPLE WITH NO CONCEPT OF THE ZOMBIE THREAT

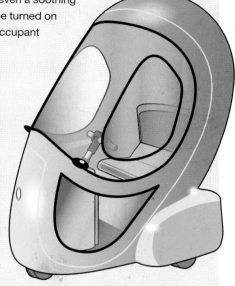

Only one problem – it might work on the computer plans but in reality this over-priced plastic dome on wheels adapts very poorly in the real world. For that price tag, you could build and equip a powerful Humvee-type Bug-Out Vehicle; instead, here you get a machine which can't help tipping over at the slightest obstruction – even a basic 4 inch kerb.

The all-around glass means you're sitting there like a mobile snack for the dead and try downloading the latest driver updates with a hungry zombie slobbering at the window. Whilst the high-tech air conditioning is draining your power, it simultaneously blows unfiltered 'human-flavour' air out, which attracts any zombie within 10 metres to your powered egg-wagon.

Finally, it is equipped with a self-drive AI which seems to veer towards large collections of the walking dead in some bizarre quirk of its on-board machine-learning algorithm.

Little real survival thinking and a major leap backwards in the personal transportation field – an area long explored by zombie survivalists. Forget this fibreglass waste of almost half a million dollars.

TRAVELLING WITH ANIMALS

Humans have been using animals for riding and carrying loads for thousands of years so it's worth considering how the animal kingdom can support your post-apocalyptic travel plans.

Before getting carried away with visions of riding into the sunset after raiding a rival survivor camp, slashing zombies with a gleaming sabre as you go, remember that although animals don't need 'fuel' they do need food, water, care and attention. Also, when we talk about animals we are looking at 2 broad areas: beasts of burden such as donkeys – used to carrying supplies – and animals you can ride, such as horses and camels.

'ANIMAL HUSBANDRY WILL BECOME A SKILL THAT IS HIGHLY VALUED IN THE POST-APOCALYPTIC WORLD'
JULIAN HENDRY, *SKILLS FOR THE END OF THE WORLD*

If you are looking at using any animal in your Bug-Out plans it's important that you have a thorough understanding of that animal's needs and capabilities, most importantly, how they react to the ever-present zombies. You will need to be experienced in the husbandry, training and care of your animals and have the necessary supplies to keep your beasts fit and healthy. One advantage that animals have is that, to date, no animal has developed the zombic condition. They can contract the virus but for reasons not yet understood, animals do not transform into zombies. The only exception is larger primates but, unless you're planning to monkey-ride your way out of the zombie wasteland, you shouldn't need to worry about luring away any zombie chimps with rotting bananas.

OPTION 1
HORSES

When considering animal transportation, horses are often the first option most survivalists consider. After all, there are almost 800,000 horses in the UK alone and training is widely available, with many stables running short intensive training sessions to help you get started. But how realistic is the horse as a post-apocalyptic form of transport? First point to note is that horses and zombies do not mix well. The rotting stench and groan of the walking dead makes them nervous and flighty. A further development is that there have been reports of zombies eating horses, although this may be to do with the presence of human scent on the animals.

Their adverse reaction to the walking dead makes them a poor choice for a zombie apocalypse. If you are considering horses, remember to get as much training as possible.

OPTION 2
PACK DONKEY

Fitted with saddlebags, working donkeys are useful pack animals and can be kept as pets providing you have the right set up. The good news is that there are thought to be over 60 million donkeys in the world. The bad news is that apart from Blackpool beach, very few of them are in the UK and Ireland. Despite being practical working animals, these robust creatures react badly to the walking dead. The lumbering motion and stench of zombies makes donkeys nervous. However, this has not stopped the Chinese Red Army investing heavily in the training of donkeys and mules as transport options, so much so that China now has more donkeys than other country.

A good option away from the walking dead. Availability is also a key factor in the UK, with less than 3,000 scattered across the country and many of these elderly and in sanctuaries.

OPTION 3
LLAMA

No quips about pan-pipes here as these South American natives are pretty useful beasts of burden. Adult male Llamas can carry around 50 kg of supplies. They also like carrots, a lot. Reports from Brazil indicate that Llamas are indifferent to the walking dead. These cool creatures aren't bothered by much and sources suggest that their strong odour masks human scent providing another layer of defence. A useful choice and a definite upgrade on the donkey in terms of reactions to the walking dead. These creatures are also adept at navigating most landscapes and can get by with very little in terms of food and water.

Seriously, Llamas really are through the looking-glass. Unless you are a professional with access to a herd, it's hard to see where you are going to source these robust animals.

TRAVELLING WITH ANIMALS
ZOMBIE RIDING – SPORT OF KINGS?

Popular in California after an outbreak in the 1880s, the infamous Raphael clan specialised in de-nailing and de-toothing zombies, then riling them up in the ring where members of the excited audience could ride the creatures rodeo style.

The powerless zombies could smell the human flesh close to them and this drove them into something of a feeding frenzy but the tragic creatures were unable to feast on it, resulting in a bucking manoeuvre, producing a realistic 'buckaroo' experience. Even if the zombies did manage to close in on a stray arm or leg, the rider would just feel a dry rasping as the zombie lacked any teeth to make the kill. This distasteful sport was banned in 1920s after a high-profile accident involving a budding 'talkie' actress, the Bishop of San Francisco and several de-toothed zombies – although several distasteful homemade video clips appear on YouTube from time to time before being quickly taken down.

WARNING! THE MINISTRY OF ZOMBIES ADVISE NEVER TO RIDE A ZOMBIE

OPTION 4
DOG SLEDS

Everyone loves dogs but a team of 6–8 Huskies? Aren't they going to eat more food than you can carry on your sled? Unless you live in the Arctic circle, dogs are costly and complex in terms of survival resources. There is specialist zombie training for dogs (see Mrs Woodford's School) and a well-trained dog can be a real asset but don't expect your household pooch to become a zombie-sniffing, ghoul biting super-dog overnight. The process takes months of training. Interestingly, experts say that any dog can pull a sled or cart with the right training and conditioning but in reality many favour larger breeds such as German Shepherds or Dobermans.

 Canines are immune to the zombic condition but keeping a team of dogs in the aftermath will be beyond most survivors. Keep them as guard dogs and companions.

OPTION 5
REINDEER SLEIGH

Here at the Ministry of Zombies, we admit we don't know much about reindeers – only that Santa uses them to pull his sleigh – so we had to call on Scandinavian survival expert Lars Amundsen. Reindeer are certainly an option in some parts of the world but you're unlikely to come across a herd if you live in Central Manchester. Amundsen claims they can carry up to 40 kg of supplies and are useful mountain walkers. The Norwegian Army has used reindeers for transport for many years and has hinted unofficially that the creatures respond well to zombies. Not a realistic option for most in the UK but may be an option for our Canadian survivalist cousins.

 Not as crazy as it sounds and everyone loves Christmas. Various military forces around the world who operate in colder climates have teams specialising in reindeer husbandry.

OPTION 6
ELEPHANTS

You might find one in a zoo but, depending on where you are in the world, it may be hard to get hold of one in an emergency situation. Also, can you imagine feeding or even hiding a fully-grown elephant? Unless you are a trained elephant expert, keep away from these majestic creatures. War elephants have been used for thousands of years and in the conquest of the Nanda Empire in 321 BC, both sides are said to have used zombie trained elephants to battle a walking dead outbreak. It's worth remembering that elephants are not counted as domesticated animals – they are in fact wild animals and this nature can make these powerful beasts unpredictable.

 There is a lot of mileage over the longer-term to recreate some zombie-busting creatures of the ancient world. Might be a better long-term project.

TRAVELLING WITH ANIMALS

MAN'S BEST FRIEND

Since the work of Mrs Victoria Woodford back in the 1970s, preppers have been aware of the use of trained dogs in survival plans. Certain breeds can be trained to sniff out the dead, attack when required and importantly are immune to developing the zombic condition, although they can be carriers of the virus. In terms of transportation, dogs are domesticated enough to travel with us, and some survivalists in northern regions have experimented with dog-sled teams, which are ideal for bugging out over long distances in icy or snowy conditions. However, in terms of carrying gear or supplies, most canines are limited to lighter items placed in specially designed panniers. The RSPCA has a small range of doggie bug out bags specially designed to carry everything a working dog will need over a 48 hour period. There is even space to add in extra water supplies and provisions to support human members of the group.

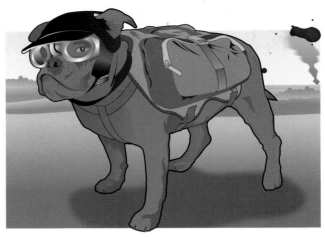

'LOOK AFTER YOUR HOUND AND THEY WILL BE BY YOUR SIDE WHATEVER CHALLENGES THE END TIMES BRING'
**MRS VICTORIA WOODFORD,
RSPCA PUBLIC LECTURE SERIES, MAY 1978**

TRAVELLING WITH ANIMALS
THE POST-APOCALYPTIC ANIMAL ENVIRONMENT

In March 2017, the Ministry of Zombies teamed up with the RSPCA to produce a draft report on how our wildlife would fare during a zombie apocalypse. For the zombie prepper, it's important to know what kind of wildlife profile you'll be facing, and also to start assessing the chances of domesticating any creatures you find roaming the wasteland. Here are the report's predictions on some of the winners and losers.

1 WILD DOGS WILL RULE

Wild dog packs will become a feature of the wasteland. With over 8 million dogs in the UK, the end of man could be the start of a new canine age. Expect wild packs of larger dogs as the smaller and domesticated ones won't last long.

2 EMPIRE OF THE RATS

Expert opinion is divided on just how many rats there are in the UK but the end of man will see a boom period for black and brown rats of every size. Numbers will expand exponentially for the first year, with the creatures growing in size and ferocity. They will head out of urban areas and die back as food runs out and they exhaust supplies.

3 CATS ON THE MENU

There are almost 7 million cats in the UK but experts predict that this won't save domesticated tabbies from becoming food. Recent tests have shown that zombies will consume cat meat if desperate, as will humans, dogs and just about everything else.

4 AN INSECT SUMMER

Imagine it, the first scorching summer with millions of dead milling around – that's paradise for flies, maggots and any number of insect pests. Expect swarms to cover parts of the country but these will die out in any colder weather.

5 WILDLIFE RETURNS

One aspect of the fall of man which 'excited' the RSPCA is that the collapse of civilisation will likely see the return of some of our endangered species – they highlight otters and barn owls as two creatures which are likely to prosper. We pointed out that everyone getting turned into zombies isn't, however, the best nature conservation scheme on offer. The report was never published.

SINAI ZOMBIE SURVIVAL CAMELS

The noble camel is truly a 'gift from God' when it comes to Bug-Out animals. Tall, strong, powerful, loyal and hardy, these animals have done good service around the world for thousands of years. In addition, camels have always been tolerant of zombies. Unlike horses, they do not find the smell of rotting flesh, the low groan or even the slashing claws of the walking dead alarming and have been used for many years in the Sinai peninsula of Egypt to battle zombies. So much so in fact that region began breeding 'zombie-resistant' camels as early as the 1900s and now such animals are available for the first time world-wide.

Genuine Sinai Zombie Survival Camels are available from the Jebaliya tribe in Egypt for as little as £1,000 plus delivery. You should be aware that you will need to meet all legal obligations for the transport and keeping of your camel and that camels generally prefer to be in groups so you may need to consider purchasing more than one. But, for now, enjoy the amazing features of this incredible animal.

These camels are fiercely loyal, particularly the females, and are dependable travelling companions, capable of travelling around 100 miles per day at an arrange speed of 3–4 mph. Although not racing camels, Jebaliya camels can reach up to 12 mph when sprinting.

'TAKE CARE OF YOUR CAMEL AND SHE WILL TAKE CARE OF YOU MY FRIEND. BE ZOMBIES OR DESERT BANDITS, SHE WILL NEVER LET YOU DOWN'
SHEIK MUSSA, JEBALIYA TRIBE, SINAI, EGYPT

FEATURES

▶ Specialised Jebaliya Zombie Saddle – enables the rider to sit high and includes various pouches for Bug-Out Supplies.

▶ The battle saddle comes with a harness for a modern version of the antique Arabic musket specially designed to fire metal anti-zombie balls. Also includes power bag and extra balls. Such a weapon is highly prized in the Sinai and is both hardy and can fire virtually anything, even pebbles.

▶ A Jebaliya camel will hiss and bash its head into zombies on command. It is more than capable of knocking ghouls to the ground and is fitted with a neat leather battle cap.

▶ These camels have been bred to give off a strong pungent odour which seems to deter the undead.

▶ Each Jebaliya camel can be upgraded with a Bedouin Bug-Out Bag – which is a high-quality low-technology survival kit, designed to pack up and fit neatly into the saddle. It includes a camping rug, goat-skin water bottle and food bag of dried fruits. It is said to be able to keep one survivor alive for several weeks.

▶ Camels are fitted with hardened shoes to cover their pads and to adapt them for urban travel. Once off tarmac, these shoes can be easily removed.

▶ Jebaliya camels do require slightly more water than other breeds but this is still substantially less than other pack or riding animals. A fully grown female can operate for up to 4 weeks without water.

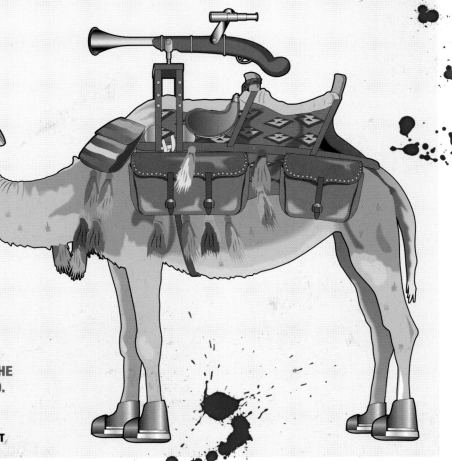

MOTORISED TRANSPORT

So far, we've reviewed some of the non-motorised transport options available but let's face it – who really wants to face the end of the world on a pair of roller skates or a scooter? The real action in the wasteland will be motorised.

Keeping and maintaining a car or other motorised vehicle could give you a real edge in the chaos – hopefully, your survival studies so far have demonstrated that. You'll be able to escape the city, forage further and outrun other hopeless and desperate survivors. This section looks at motorised prepping with particular reference to creating a safe location for your vehicle and includes detailed plans on converting the 'average family car' into a post-apocalyptic road warrior machine. Many of the guidelines are equally applicable to other vehicle types so feel free to adapt and develop your own ideas as far as your budget and skills will allow. Technology is consumer demand driven so we now regularly see innovative cross-overs in the marketplace such as expensive branded luxury cars that have impressive off-road credentials, including full 4 wheel drive, despite never leaving the city.

In reality, it would be impossible to include every possible configuration of motorised transport in this manual so we will start with a broad survey of 'car-type' vehicles before looking at larger vehicles such as vans, coaches and buses later in the volume. For now, let's review the most common types of vehicles found on our roads such as sports, passenger, classic and the growing category of sports utility vehicles, as well as hardy pickup trucks and flexible people carriers.

OPTION 1
SPORTS CARS

High performance sports and soft top 2 seaters won't survive long in the wastelands. They may look the business and, for sure, the end of the world is the time to snag a test drive from that deserted supercar showroom in Mayfair, but that's all it will be – a short test drive. Delicate, highly tuned engines, extremely low ground-clearance and poor storage – there's not much for a serious zombie prepper to love here. Blocked and uneven roads will negate the only advantage they do offer – their exceptional acceleration and speed.

 You may occasionally see them driven by warlords as trophies and demonstrations of power but apart from that, they'll disappear pretty quickly. Plus, driving an open top car during a zombie outbreak is like sticking a sign on your head saying 'please eat me'.

OPTION 2
FAMILY HATCHBACKS

Lists like this can sometimes seem like a catalogue selection from which you select the right option for you and to some extent this is the case. But, for many, the humble family car will be their vehicle of choice for obvious reasons. One of these is that it's one of the most common car types on the road and this means most survivors will be familiar with the layout and operation. They're also a good balance of storage, passenger space and power. However, modern family cars are designed for tarmac roads and often perform badly off-road or in poor road conditions.

 This broad group of vehicles will be the choice of thousands of survivors but it's important to look at some of the adaptations reviewed in this book to turn a reasonable zombie survival car into a hardened zombie-proof Bug-Out Vehicle.

OPTION 3
EMERGENCY VEHICLES

A wide range of options, some with the mouth-watering prospect of firearms and other specialist equipment you can turn on the walking dead. At the end of the world, who would pass up the opportunity to grab an emergency vehicle and 'blue light' it through the wasteland? There are some serious choices here in terms of ambulances, police cars and even SWAT team vehicles. Many models are adapted for emergency conditions and don't overlook the well-equipped command and control vehicles.

 First things first – if an emergency vehicle is still in use you must leave it. Many first-responders will be desperately battling to save humanity; the last thing they want is their vehicle getting stolen or looted. Wait to find an abandoned model.

MOTORISED TRANSPORT
THE ROAD, LAW AND ZOMBIES

Much of the advice in this manual focuses on vehicle choice and careful preparation – but what if you find yourself without transport during a zombie outbreak? The Ministry of Zombies asked a prominent expert about the legalities of 'procuring' transport during a crisis.

▶ The first consideration must be whether the governing authority has declared an official state of emergency. If this has been done, then the standard UN rules around the legality of foraging apply.

▶ Secondly, is whether procuring a vehicle from a zombie constitutes legal theft – in many legal codes around the world a human turned into a zombie is still, at least legally, considered to be alive. If you find the perfect vehicle with a zombie inside, then you deal with the zombie and make off with the said vehicle, you could be guilty of theft.

All clear? In reality, the legal guidelines around a major zombie outbreak are complex and unclear. Far better to be prepared but if you do find yourself in dire straits remember to forage only what you need to get back to your home base, do no harm to your fellow survivors and be wary of rogues or bandits posing as police or other authorities.

OPTION 4
SUVs

Sports Utility Vehicles (SUVs) now dominate our roads, with some models offering car-like levels of comfort with real off-road capability. A solid 4WD version from a good manufacturer is a superb base for your zombie survival planning. SUVs are hard wearing, have good storage and a high driving position – all good assets for apocalyptic driving. Not the best fuel economy – some models are prone to tipping over – and be cautious of models which are designed to have the 'look' of an SUV but come with no off-road capability.

 An SUV or Jeep is a very practical choice but be wary as not all SUV's are the same. Many preppers favour slightly older models, which deliver a rougher ride but have less of the on-board technology disliked by serious survivalists.

OPTION 5
PICKUP TRUCKS

Hardy workhorses, designed for tough conditions – what's not to love? Superb build quality, decent off-road capability and ample storage. Basic models are tough enough, although many lack the comforts of a car, but top-level models are possibly the best production model vehicles for the end of the world. The Toyota Hilux Invincible rules the pickup world. There is little this vehicle cannot do. Technology levels are creeping up on these vehicles so older models may be easy to maintain. Source an older model in good condition if you can.

 Later in this volume, we'll take a look at commercial vehicles as potential Bug-Out options. Many light commercial vehicles share the same features as pickup trucks but for many reasons, pickups seem to be the vehicle of choice for hardcore preppers.

OPTION 6
PEOPLE CARRIERS

Most frequently seen on the school run, these vehicles are often referred to by preppers as 'Road Utility Vehicles' or RUVs. There are countless variations and makes, from smaller 6-seaters all the way up to converted commercial vehicle minibuses. Their obvious strength is storage space and the capacity to transport a group in one. Add to this that many models offer good performance and fuel economy. The downside is off-road performance with most production models managing very poorly on anything other than smooth tarmac roads.

 Standard models offer excellent storage capacity and should be considered if you plan to make your 'daily use' car into your Bug-Out Vehicle. Shares many of the limitations of a family car in terms of going off-road.

MOTORISED TRANSPORT

CONVERTING YOUR CAR

One of the more frequent questions asked on zombie prepper forums is 'How can I prepare my car for the zombie apocalypse?' The query is often followed up with the information that many people only have one car and that it's used for the daily school run. So, how can you practically prepare your vehicle?

1 TIME AND RESOURCES

From that first moment when you wake up to find slobbering zombies at your window to when you're a fully prepared zombie prepper, time and resources are a key consideration. How serious are you about zombie prepping? What kind of money and time are you prepared to put into staying safe?

2 VEHICLE SELECTION

You may own a battle-equipped Humvee or a 2001 Rover which is forever breaking down – you need to get the 'core' right if you are going to invest in your vehicle. How robust is your current vehicle? Is it suitable as a framework for your anti-zombie preparation plans?

3 DEFENSIVE ARMOUR

Selecting the right armour to defend your vehicle is vital – fit a fully high-tech armour plate to resist any raiders or use chicken wire across the windows. Are you prepared to be known as the 'village nutcase' if you fit a steel grill across your windscreen? Heavy armour can also impact on fuel efficiency – have you budgeted for this?

4 WEAPONS AND ARMAMENT

Known as 'tooling up' in the prepper community, it could be using anything from a spare M60 you had lying around the garage to a box of plastic forks that were left over after Grandad's 70th. Do you understand what you can legally do in terms of adding weapons to your vehicle? Are you confident you can handle any new firepower that you fit?

This schematic overviews the key anti-zombie and apocalypse features which can be fitted to a standard family car. It outlines the main zones of operation when it comes to fixtures and fittings which will help you stay alive in the wasteland.

FENDERS, BONNET

There are many options to strengthen your front corners, particularly if you plan to hit a lot of zombies – consider wrapping with bull bars and additional soldered plates. The bonnet can be used as a weapons platform but fitting is considerably more complicated than roof versions. Some preppers simply cover their bonnet with small sandbags to protect the engine area.

DOORS

Modern car doors are sufficient to keep out the walking dead but you may want to strengthen in case of any road war damage – consider collision shields, welded plates or spikes. It is important that your vehicle has an alternative escape route other than the 2–4 main doors, perhaps through the boot or out of the top.

ROOF

Often referred to as 'the deck' in zombie vehicle prepping circles – ensure that you have a properly constructed hatch whether you plan to use it for observation, escape or as a weapons platform – consider adding mounted weapons, directional lights and zombie-whistles. Also a useful location for storage.

WHEELS AND ARCHES

A protective skirt around your wheel arches is a good investment and can be relatively easy to fit. In some cases, these can be fitted to almost cover the wheel. In terms of tyres, consider an apocalypse-grade tyre. Opinion is divided on the subject of wheel blades – with many survivors saying that they are more dangerous to your own party than the walking dead. Still, it would look cool to have great half-metre blades spinning from the wheels.

COLOUR

Are zombies colour sensitive? The medical evidence is inconclusive but what evidence we do have suggests they are drawn to brighter colours. Also, think hiding in an urban landscape, not sticking out. Look at dark colours, greys, mottled and dirty, painted on rust – urban camouflage means you won't be an obvious target.

MINISTRY OF ZOMBIES

FRONT GRILL

Many SUVs already have them but your front bumper needs to be replaced by a full-range bull bar system. Look out for a modern polyethylene one which is still hardy enough for zombie bashing but will offer some spring and deflect defence in the event of a collision. The front of your vehicle will certainly require protection in this area. It is not unheard of for a particularly sharp fragment of zombie bone to pierce the grill of a regular car and do some serious damage, so defend your front.

WINDSHIELD

Modern windscreens are strong but this area should still be protected by some form of cage. Ensure that it doesn't block your wipers and consider fitting improved blades to help you clear the excessive zombie matter from the screen. Halfords will be selling a 'zombie-cleaning' screen wash from 2020 onwards but you'll need to order specialist screen wash online until then – choose the purple-coloured ZombAway screen wash).

OTHER WINDOWS

Modern vehicle glass is strong enough to resist zombies but you may still want to supplement it with steel mesh. If you are going for full armour then consider bulletproof glass or steel shutters. Darkened glass can help avoid any unwanted zombie attention plus gives you that 'street gangsta' look.

GENERAL ARMOUR

There are various levels of car armour so get some specialist advice. B4 or B6 ballistic protection levels will be sufficient for most hostile wasteland encounters. Many preppers defend key areas so as not to overload the vehicle. It's not cheap to armour up a car.

MOTORISED TRANSPORT

VEHICLE INTERIOR

Maintaining your vehicle's interior systems, such as your on-board Bug-Out Supply, which will help keep you mobile and alive in the wasteland, is a core requirement – never overlook it! Think of the interior of your vehicle as your mobile survival space. It's the location you will come to rely on for keeping the supplies and weapons that will keep you alive. In truth, you could fill a whole volume on both topics but in this section, we'll just do a quick survey of the key issues and challenges.

There are various techniques for creating additional space in an average car, the most obvious being to remove any unnecessary seating, particularly at the rear. With new models, vehicle designers go to great lengths to create 'unique' vehicle interiors and most lack configurable options – for example, central consoles can rarely be moved as they conceal crucial electrical or mechanical components vital to the car's functioning. Realistically, any work beyond seat removal or creating interior access to the boot could end up more costly than just buying a more suitable Bug-Out Vehicle.

▶ BUG-OUT VEHICLE BOOT

The list included here is very much an idealised Bug-Out Boot example. Does your on-board Bug-Out Kit need to be in the boot? No. We have already looked at the option of using a trailer but, for most people, the boot is a logical location. Remember, Bug-Out supplies are a personal choice but should contain everything you need to stay on the road and survive. You will most likely need to re-work the following suggestions based on factors such as the size of your vehicle and group, your budget and any legal requirements.

⚠ IMPORTANT

ALWAYS ADHERE TO THE CURRENT LAWS AND REGULATIONS AROUND ROAD VEHICLE WORTHINESS, INSURANCE AND THE CARRYING OF WEAPONS. IT'S POINTLESS CREATING YOUR DREAM ZOMBIE APOCALYPSE VEHICLE FROM GRANDMA'S OLD COROLLA ONLY TO HAVE IT SEIZED BY THE 'FEDS' BEFORE THE DEAD RISE. BE DISCREET. GET YOURSELF EDUCATED AND STAY LEGAL.

1 FULL-SIZED SPARE TYRE

Forget space-saving alternatives, a full-sized spare tyre with the appropriate floor jack is an essential component in any on-board Bug-Out Supplies. A flat or punctured tyre is possibly the top reason for vehicle breakdown so be prepared with the parts, tools and the skills to complete a change. You should be able to change your vehicle's tyre in less than 10 minutes.

2 DRINKING WATER/PURIFICATION KIT

Again, a vital part of any kit. Experts suggest at least a gallon a day per survivor of drinking water, supported by purification kits and tablets. Commercially bottled mineral water will last about 3 years but most hardcore survivalists prefer to bottle their own in bulk containers adding a preservative such as tiny quantities of household bleach. You should only use this technique once you are confident in your own survival skills.

3 FUEL SUPPLIES

It is a golden rule to always keep your vehicle fuel tank topped up. You should also keep on-board supplies in purpose-built jerry cans. Consider the use of preservatives such as fuel stabilisers to increase the longevity of your fuel and keep your stocks in rotation. Writing dates clearly on cans will help with this.

4 EMERGENCY BUG-OUT BAG

If you have less than a minute to abandon your vehicle or if it breaks down and you have to get out in a hurry, this is the backpack you grab. 72 hours of essential supplies in a light-weight back pack. Grab it, grab your weapon and get your skates on. Remember that you may be able to return to your vehicle once it's safe to do so to forage more supplies.

5 WEAPONS CACHE

Every survivor on-board will be carrying weapons so this is your extra cache of weapons and ammunition. Our illustration shows an adapted AK-47z assault rifle plus side arms. Where firearms are restricted for legal reasons, consider pepper spray, baseball bats, police-style batons. Weapons mix is a personal choice so consider those in your party and your defence requirements.

6 ALTERNATIVE TRANSPORT

In our example, there's an inflatable boat as an alternative Bug-Out Vehicle. This is a practical choice as it doesn't take up much room and is particularly useful where the collapse of civilisation has led to wide scale flooding. Other interior solutions could include folding bicycles or small handcarts, the latter being used to ferry supplies away from an abandoned vehicle.

MOTORISED TRANSPORT
INTERIOR CABIN

Everything inside your vehicle must justify its space so strip back on any unnecessary gadgets and electrics. You need as much space as possible for armed crew, weapons and any supplies. If you don't need all the seats, consider removing them. Many preppers have their vehicle strengthened with internal support bars, to create a strong crash-proof cage inside. Don't forget some secret compartments for essentials.

Most survivalists create a system with their full Bug-Out supplies in the boot and with further smaller bags or kits inside the cabin. This decision depends on many factors including the vehicle and your plans once the walking dead arrive. There are any number of accessories you can spend your survival budget on to enhance your vehicle such as military grade navigation systems with pre-downloaded maps, encrypted two-way radios but don't overlook a good library of national maps and a compass. Check any decent survival forum for hundreds of posts on the various bits of post-apocalyptic technology now out there on the market.

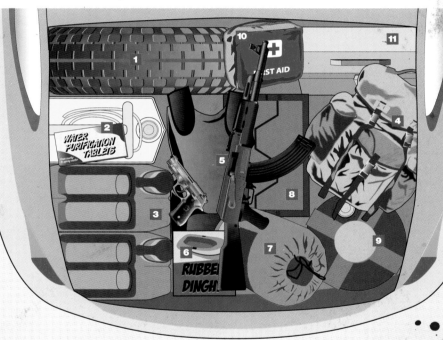

7 SLEEPING BAG AND TEMPORARY SHELTER

This set of items should be scaled according to the size of your party. For sure, a 5-seasons sleeping bag with a good-sized green plastic sheet is the minimum. If you have the space, add in more plastic sheets with rope.

8 CONCEALED STORAGE SPACE

Some vehicles have useful under-boot storage areas. It's worth sourcing a Bug-Out Vehicle with this feature as it can be used to store anything you want to be over-looked by a quick and opportunistic thief. Some preppers install booby traps inside these areas.

9 SEALED CONTAINERS

Tough plastic containers are excellent locations in which to store emergency rations as well any other emergency kit such as fire lighting equipment and cooking utensils. There is vast wealth of information out there about Bug-Out food selections but obviously long-duration is a key factor. There is also a debate on the use of 'ready-to-eat' emergency rations, which are widely used in the military and take up minimal space.

10 MEDICAL KIT

Again, plenty of discussion on the content of an Emergency Bug-Out Kit but remember to get the training to support anything you include. A basic kit should have basic medical supplies but also personal hygiene products such as antibacterial wet wipes, which can help reduce the chances of infection, and any prescription medicines you need. An emergency dental kit is also worth investigating.

11 SPARES AND PARTS

Tyres and jacks have already been mentioned but the list of what to include is still endless – consider spare batteries, jump cables, basic tools, fuses, fan belts and fluids. It's also worth including emergency lighting and the relevant Haynes car manual, along with any other survival material you can't live without.

MOTORISED TRANSPORT

ENGINE AND MECHANICS

Experts often refer to keeping your vehicle in 'good working order' and, in this sense, preparing your vehicle for the zombie apocalypse is no exception – every vehicle be it a car, SUV or motorcycle requires regular maintenance, particularly to core drive areas such as the engine. Running out of fuel, an over-heated engine or even a flat battery are no longer minor inconveniences in the wasteland – these kind of vehicle issues could get you eaten. Whilst it may be tempting to start steel meshing windows and fitting killer zombie bull bars to the front of your car, never overlook the maintenance of these parts of your vehicle.

In terms of car performance, preparing a Bug-Out Vehicle is less about delicate fine-tuning to improve acceleration or top speed and more about ensuring you get the best fuel economy possible, that your engine continues to function and there is less wear on components such as tyres. One important factor to consider, and which runs counter to some of the survival features reviewed in this book, is assessing your vehicle's ideal weight – strip out any unnecessary clutter and weight to maximise your MPG. It's remarkable how often vehicles fitted with the latest anti-zombie weapons breakdown at survival training events for reasons linked to a simple lack of maintenance. Keep your car healthy with the best oil, quality air filters, regularly changed spark plugs and the best tyres you can afford.

 ## MOTORISED TRANSPORT
VEHICLE CHECKS

Remember the basics from your zombie survival training – keep the fluids and fuel topped up; keep the engine and mechanics well-maintained; regularly check for any blockages, particularly as zombie gunk tends to bung up filters. Maintaining your vehicle can be summarised using the acronym FITBOW – these go beyond just considering the engine so it's best to think of FITBOW as a complete check of the automotive survival system rather than just a basic engine check.

 ### FLUIDS
Fuel, windscreen washer (zombie variant if possible) and coolant. Basic stuff but the cause of many breakdowns if not regularly checked, particularly if you've been under fire.

 ### INTERIOR
Basic check on Bug-Out Supplies – is everything topped up and in date. Are your weapons clean and maintained? Is your interior clean, tidy and secure?

ALWAYS KEEP YOUR VEHICLE WELL-MAINTAINED, SERVICED AND TOPPED UP WITH FLUIDS AND FUEL. NO ONE WANTS A VEHICLE BREAK DOWN JUST AS THE HORDE IS DESCENDING

 ### TYRES
Check pressure and your spare. Look out for any stray zombie bone shards or other damage to the rims. Regularly check on your jack and any tools you plan to use for changing a wheel.

 ### BASHERS
Bashers is a term mainly used in the US to refer to any fixed or on-board weapons. If you've fitted a frontal grill, is it fixed and firmly held in place? Check any anti-zombie weapons such as decomposition filters etc.

 ### OIL
Oil should get a special mention. In reality, survivors are good at checking fuel levels but they forget to check their oil. Easy to check and easy to top up but let it run down or get a leak and miss it and you can do irreparable damage to your vehicle.

 ### WINDOWS
Check for cracks and that any steel mesh is firmly in place. Keep your windows clear and clean. Zombie gunk from creatures you run down will smother your windscreen, blocking your view and leaving masses of infected material on the vehicle. Clean it down with watered-down bleach before using any window cleaning products.

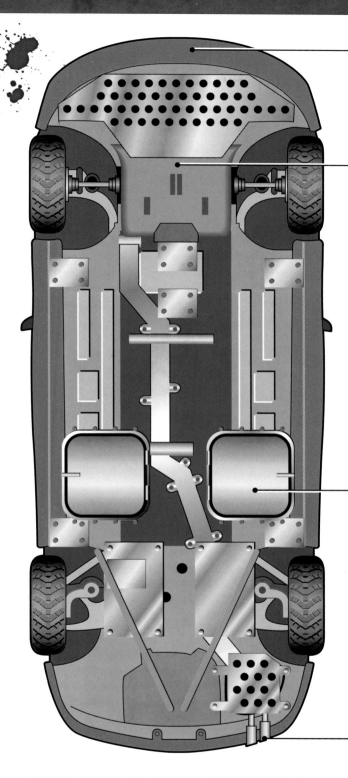

GROUND CLEARANCE

You need good ground clearance for any off-road driving and many preppers opt to support this by insisting that their Bug-Out Vehicle is a robust 4WD model.

SHIELDING

It is possible to shield the underside of your vehicle and therefore reduce both the number of grab points for zombies and off-road damage by fitting steel skid plates. Not all experts agree on the need for under-body armour.

ESCAPE HATCH

Fitting a vehicle floor exit hatch is a major adjustment but can be worth it on a larger vehicle. On smaller vehicles, survivors tend to look at the cheaper option of escaping through the back seat and the boot. Also, as any automotive engineer will tell you, unless professionally done, any structural alterations to your vehicle will affect the strength of the car-frame – most of which are now in a 'unibody' construction format. Basically, you don't want to make any changes that could weaken your vehicle in the event of a roll-over or if you are planning to add body armour or weapons.

'END OF THE WORLD' EXHAUST

Your exhaust system needs some special attention for two reasons. Firstly, from a defensive perspective, it will need reinforcing or a combination of grabbing zombies and off-road driving will take its toll. Secondly, going on the offensive, it is worth fitting a decomposition kit weapon system to your vehicle. Both adjustments will cost money but are very worthwhile investments. Beyond this, a regular maintenance routine should be in place to monitor the system and check on noise levels. Most serious zombie preppers keep a complete spare exhaust system in their fortified garage. It's a relatively inexpensive insurance policy against any major issues.

REMEMBER
Excessive noise from a poorly maintained vehicle or a noisy diesel engine will attract the dead from every street corner. All engines make noise but in zombie survival terms – the quieter the better.

'ADDING ANY PLATE ARMOUR UNDERNEATH YOUR VEHICLE WILL ADD WEIGHT AND ISN'T ALWAYS EFFECTIVE. THE REAL ANSWER TO BETTER OFF-ROAD PERFORMANCE IS GETTING GOOD GROUND CLEARANCE, YOUR APPROACH AND DEPARTURE ANGLES RIGHT, PLENTY OF LOW END TORQUE AND THE RIGHT TYRES'
TONY 'WINKLE' HODGETTS, FORMER RAC PATROLMAN AND ZOMBIE SURVIVALIST

MOTORISED TRANSPORT

FITTED WEAPONS

It's incorrect to define 'fitted weapons' as permanent on-board fixtures to your vehicle as in practice many can be removed if need be. For example, if you are forced to abandon your perfect zombie Bug-Out Vehicle, you can still detach the specially configured M60z you mounted on the roof, providing that you can carry it. However, there is permanence around many fitted weapons, particularly the offensive capability items such as fixed front guns and rear-flame tail guns. There are also important legal regulations to consider. Under current UK law, you cannot equip your vehicle with any of the weapons mentioned in this manual – bar having a bag of baseball bats in the boot – and still be 'street legal'. You are therefore left with an important decision to make – do you adapt your vehicle now or, if you plan to continue to use it on a daily basis, do you make any amendments closer to Z-Day? Alternatively, if you have the budget, you could purchase a second vehicle especially for zombie apocalypse conversion purposes.

THE GOLDEN RULES

If you are 'tooling up' your vehicle, there are some golden rules you need to consider before you even start. The first relates to weight and over-loading your vehicle ('weapons platform' in survival speak). The second is about blending in and not standing out. The third relates to getting your hands on whatever firepower you can. If there was a further rule, it would be to practice with your vehicle – only in this way can you iron out any issues with your weaponry.

- ▶ Body armour on the wrong vehicle will drastically slow you down. Ensure that you have the right base vehicle and then improve as appropriate. Manage the weight of your vehicle very carefully during any conversion process.
- ▶ Don't overlook the benefit of your vehicle blending in. A dirty, bashed up and non-descript exterior is ideal if you, for example, leave it parked as you go off foraging. Consider therefore whether to fit your M60z now or keep it hidden on the back seat until needed.
- ▶ Not easy in the UK but you need to get your hands on some 'firepower' to put raiders off and defend against the dead. Think guns, crossbows and any ranged weapons, supported by your standard clubbing weapons. You cannot rely on defensive weapons alone – you must be able to project your attacks if required.

▶ ROOF MOUNTED MACHINE GUN

There are many ways to add firepower to your vehicle, with many hardcore preppers preferring two bonnet mounted machine or rail guns. But if you're new to this and are thinking about converting your family car then a roof mounted option is the best place to start. Your first port of call should be to ensure that you have a sunroof fitted. If you don't, you'll need one. Even if you do, a standard fitted sunroof is not sufficient to mount weapons such as the popular M60z. It is worth getting a professional to create the weapons sub-structure as an unstable platform can render this powerful weapon almost useless. In most configurations, at least one seat is removed from the interior to make space for an integrated ammunition box and belt feed.

'FOR MOST UK DRIVERS, FIREARMS ARE HARD TO SOURCE AT BEST AND IN MANY CASES ILLEGAL. SURVIVALISTS NEED TO GET CREATIVE. DON'T OVERLOOK THE POTENTIAL OF ITEMS SUCH AS NAIL-GUNS AND FRONTAL SCOOPS'
MICK 'FROSTY' HILLS, ZOMBIE SURVIVALIST, EX-SAS TROOPER

▶ REAR-FLAME TAIL GUN

This is where things get toasty and serious. Flame throwing weapons are dangerous to use and deploy but can be devastating against the walking dead. This unit can only be ordered in the US at the moment and isn't cheap – a kit costs around £3,000 plus fitting and a day's training. However, imagine the feeling when you 'fry up' a horde of zombies who are chasing your vehicle or when you scare off a gang of would-be looters with a puff of flame. Not for the faint-hearted, fitting a rear-flame weapon could be invaluable to clear off any pursuing hordes or 'enemy' vehicles but it's a serious investment, plus some experts consider the danger of carrying the flame-fuel on board to be enough of a risk to outweigh the obvious 'street cred' benefits.

'A FLAME WEAPON IS NOT FOR EVERYONE – IT'S A SERIOUS PIECE OF KIT AND REQUIRES FITTING BY A SPECIALIST. THERE ARE SO MANY WAYS IT COULD ALL GO WRONG. WIND BLOWS THE FLAME THE WRONG WAY – GAME OVER'
TONY 'WINKLE' HODGETTS, FORMER RAC PATROLMAN AND ZOMBIE SURVIVALIST

1 A circular steel rack is fitted on top to ensure all angles around the vehicle can be covered. Access is through an armoured roof hatch.

2 The schematic shows a complete tubular steel substructure has been created in this vehicle to provide a stable firing platform for the gun above. Such a frame cannot just be bolted to the roof or existing restraints. A more robust substructure ensures that the weapon can be fired whilst on the move.

3 An optional automatic feed-way links to an ammunition box within the vehicle, providing 600-900 anti-ghoul dum-dum rounds.

4 The M... in this schematic will fire a... ...minute, low... ...issue your master!

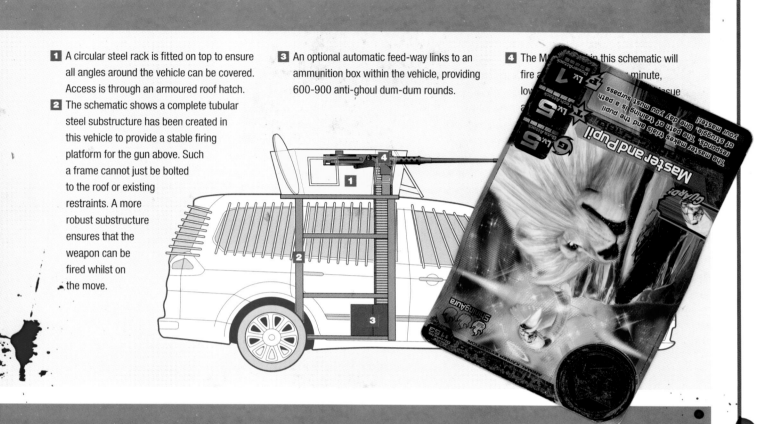

The master makes trials and the pupil responds. The path of training is a path of struggle. One day you must surpass your master!

Master and Pupil!

1 Most rear-flame tail guns are fitted with the igniter unit extending from underneath the bumper behind the vehicle to a distance of around 10 cm. This clearance is important for safety reasons.

2 Some models are disguised as down-pointing exhaust pipes and 'fry up' the ground behind the vehicle – these variations have an automatic igniter safety catch which is enabled when the vehicle is stationary.

3 Your flame-fuel reserve is typically inside the boot, with a controlling unit in the cabin, enabling those inside to switch the weapon on for short bursts of up to 3 seconds.

4 A standard unit with a full flame-fuel load is capable of around 10 such 3 second bursts, sending flames up to 10 metres to the rear of the vehicle.

MOTORISED TRANSPORT

ON-BOARD WEAPONS

Storing firearms or any kind of weapon in your vehicle will present challenges. Most obvious of all of course is that your vehicle will not be street legal with a fitted rear-flame thrower and an M60 sticking out of a firing port on the roof. However, there are also guidelines you should follow when keeping weapons in a confined space such as keeping any Bug-Out Weapons in a secure and locked case when not on 'missions', using safety catches where appropriate and ensuring that anyone using a weapon, be it your M60, a baseball bat with barbed wire and nail accessories or a cricket bat, is trained and competent to use it in combat. All sounds like common sense but

remember that survival experts estimate that almost 20% of all prepper causalities in any emergency are victims of unintentional wounds inflicted using their own weapons.

▶ DECOMPOSITION FILTER OR 'DECOMP KIT'

A specialist piece of anti-zombie kit that can be fitted to virtually any exhaust pipe. A decent 'Decomp' kit will typically cost around £300 but is a very worthwhile investment. It can be fitted with no visible impact and does not affect the emission standards of your vehicle during any MOT testing. Just remember not to leave the dead scent filter on or the garage could end up with some very strange results. Most units come with full instructions and can be fitted without the need for specialist tools. It is worth checking vehicle compatibility online before ordering as most filters won't fit very new cars or heavy goods vehicles.

1 The base unit is fitted to the underside of the vehicle. In most configurations, it is between the catalytic converter and the muffler. (Warning – a decomposition unit is not a replacement for the catalytic converter.)

2 Inside the base unit, there are several cells, each of which contains replaceable chemical pellets. Typically, there are 3 units on each side – the dead pellets and the live pellets.

3 The unit is controlled from within the cabin. Activate the dead cells and your vehicle will leave a trail of 'zombie scent' behind it. When stationary, the dead scent fills the air and the dead become disinterested and shamble off.

4 Equally, activate the living cell and the dead will be drawn to you, enabling you to build up a tail of following zombies. Useful for clearing an area or offensive operations against fellow survivors.

CONTROL UNIT
Different makers produce different control units but most have three settings for your filter. 'Off' indicates no activity from the unit, exhaust fumes will flow through as per normal. 'Dead' activates one of the cells within the unit to release zombie-like dead scent. The 'Live' similarly releases a live-flesh scent.

⚠ IMPORTANT

ALWAYS TAKE INTO ACCOUNT THAT FUMES IN THE AIR ARE AFFECTED BY ENVIRONMENTAL FACTORS – FOR EXAMPLE, THE FILTERS PERFORM POORLY WHEN MOVING AT SPEED OR IN WINDY CONDITIONS AND ARE VIRTUALLY USELESS IN THE RAIN.

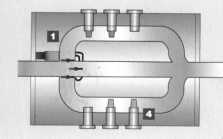

PACK 1
THE ESSENTIALS
STAY STREET LEGAL BUT STILL ZOMBIE RESISTANT

Pack 1 contains key elements familiar to any survivalist or prepper and focuses on keeping your vehicle street legal (just) and will drastically improve your general disaster and zombie preparedness. If you are on a limited budget or restricted to one car then this pack of survival goodies is where you start. Much of it is common sense and will fit discreetly into most cars. It should be supported by a full maintenance schedule for the vehicle and remember to rotate any water and food in your Bug-Out Supplies. Importantly, ensure that you run regular tests with your vehicle. One exercise could be to run through the house at 02.00 am screaming about zombies. Get the rest of the family into the car and practice bugging out by driving 100 miles up the motorway. Can your family survive on your Bug-Out supplies alone? Given time, they will certainly appreciate the benefits of your early morning training regime.

- ▶ Fully equipped Bug-Out Boot Pack
- ▶ Basic tool and spares kit
- ▶ Plastic sheeting and emergency shelter
- ▶ Jerry can of fuel (with rotation plan)
- ▶ Hand pump and siphon
- ▶ Extra clothing pack
- ▶ Emergency food and water (48 hours for 4 people)
- ▶ Basic first aid kit
- ▶ Street legal weapons

PACK 2
ZOMBIE DEFENCE BASICS
FUN ZOMBIE-BUSTING STUFF FOR ALL DRIVERS

This is where things get spicy. Zombies aren't good at getting into cars but there are some basic improvements you can make to move your vehicle from 'zombie-proof' to 'zombie-killa'. Pack 2 hovers in that grey area between almost legal and 'I'm sorry officer I had no idea there was a flame-thrower in my boot.' It includes basics such as having a mesh grill over the windows and mean looking frontal bull bars that are going to get you noticed on the school run. If you're serious about preparing your vehicle for the zombie apocalypse then this is the time to consider buying a second vehicle and turning it into your primary Bug-Out Vehicle. Remember that items such as a razor-sharp cutting scoop and vehicle mounted flare guns will mean your vehicle failing its MOT and will therefore impact on your insurance premiums.

- ▶ Front steel bull bars
- ▶ Additional cage protection bars around the corners and rear
- ▶ Metal mesh protective cover on all windows
- ▶ Floor hatch to provide emergency exit
- ▶ Front-fitted zombie scoop
- ▶ Decomposition filter on the exhaust
- ▶ Rear-Flame Tail Gun (optional)
- ▶ Vehicle mounted flare array

PACK 3
THE ROAD WARRIOR
AND FINALLY, THINGS GET SERIOUS

Pack 3 will transform your vehicle from a zombie defence machine into a set of wheels in which you can dominate the wasteland. It involves major changes where appropriate to accommodate an array of weapons and on-board defences. Most vehicles at this level will be SUVs, pickups or larger cars but it is possible to convert a smaller passenger car – you will just have to consider the power-weight ratio or you will end up with an under-performing vehicle and a chronic over-heating problem. In this volume, you'll find items such as roof-mounted M60s and rear-vehicle flamers – in fact, there are thousands of variations of weapons you can fit to your Bug-Out Vehicle. Add to this full car body armour and bulletproof glass. Pack 1 prepares you for survival. Pack 2 for the zombies. Pack 3 is not only about defending yourself against the growing threat of human bandits but also about having the kind of vehicle to support a new lifestyle in the wasteland.

- ▶ Vehicle structure strengthening – steel bar support body pack
- ▶ Armalite apocalypse car-body armour (where vehicle allows)
- ▶ Armalite bulletproof glass to all windows
- ▶ Fuel tank booster (armoured)
- ▶ On-board firearms cabinet
- ▶ Roof-mounted firearms (optional)
- ▶ Additional storage space (involves seat removal)

MOTORISED TRANSPORT

THE PERFECT ZOMBIE APOCALYPSE VEHICLE

It's important not to get over-whelmed by the hundreds of Bug-Out or apocalypse vehicles on offer and the countless variations and improvements you can make to boost your survival chances. Think of this manual as a work book, packed with ideas – some of which will work for you, others which won't. Every survivor has a unique plan when it comes to transportation during a zombie apocalypse, and no two Bug-Out systems are the same. Indeed many preppers keep their own plans under wraps for obvious reasons. However, in the diverse and bizarre world of zombie survival, there are some individuals who do speak out and who freely share information and plans with the general aim of increasing humanity's preparedness for a zombie outbreak.

Crown Prince Hussein Bin Abdullah of Jordon is one such person and has used his own fortune to actively sponsor zombie survival initiatives all over the world.

▶ THE ZOM 90E ROAD WARRIOR (PROTOTYPE)

Nothing is perfect – at least that's what they say – and they may be right but this ghoul-busting prototype car comes pretty close. With currently only 5 in existence, it's going to be hard to get your grubby hands on but it's worth reading the features list alone for the countless innovations and ideas included to help the driver survive and even prosper in a wasteland littered with the walking dead and human bandits. The car comes out of a famous automotive lab in Amman, Jordan, where scientists and engineers from across the region have been working together to create a gold-standard zombie survival vehicle.

'MY WHOLE OBJECTIVE WITH THIS VEHICLE WAS TO CREATE A PROTOTYPE WHICH CAN BE SHOWN TO MOTOR MANUFACTURERS AROUND THE WORLD. I'VE HAD PROMISING MEETINGS WITH A MAJOR MANUFACTURER ALREADY – MAINLY ABOUT THE POSSIBILITY OF CONVERTING THE ZOM 90E INTO A STREET LEGAL MASS-PRODUCED CAR, WHICH PREPPERS COULD THEN ADD TO AS THE NEED ARISES'
CROWN PRINCE HUSSEIN BIN ABDULLAH

THE ZOM 90E ROAD WARRIOR
Manufactured by the Royal Jordanian Automotive Consortium, currently with 5 versions of the 90E in discussion. Technical plans available on request.

PURPOSE
The ultimate road-warrior vehicle designed to rule the wasteland and be tough enough to fight off both zombies and any human aggressors.

TECHNICAL SPECIFICATIONS
This model is based on a seriously upgraded Hyundai Veloster Turbo. The model is a 4-door hatchback armed with a blistering 1.8 custom bi-fuel compatible TCi GDi engine. The transmission is a 7-speed automatic DCT. Importantly, the team wanted to use a production car as a base for the 90E, with another of the prototypes built on the frame of a Toyota Hilux, and another using an ex-police force Honda CR-V.

ARMAMENTS
These vehicles really pack a punch. The primary weapon is a swivel M60 which is accessed via a roof hatch. The secondary armament consists of twin experimental IWI Negev 7.64mm machine guns mounted on each wing. The twin Negevs can be directed from within the cabin. Additional weapons include a zombie leg slicing chainsaw.

RANGE
The Hyundai variant has a range of around 400 miles, which can be increased by use of an additional internal tank to 500 miles. It achieves up to 30 miles per gallon, which is impressive given its level of armour and weaponry.

CREW
The vehicle can carry 4 survivors, complete with Bug-Out Supplies and weapons but 3 is more comfortable for long-distance travel.

BUDGET
Not released. Experts estimate a budget of around £80,000. Also worth considering is Toyota and Honda variations which reports indicate both come in at under £60,000. (These estimates exclude firearm and ammunition costs.)

USAGE GUIDELINES
The ZOM 90E is a punchy and fast ride ideally suited to navigating the wasteland after the fall of civilisation. Its gearing gives it excellent acceleration and the steering is responsive and the car manoeuvrable. You can defend yourself against most opponents and the all-round armour means that it's possible to carry out ram-raids, making use of the roof or back exit to procure supplies without having to venture outside and face the zombies.

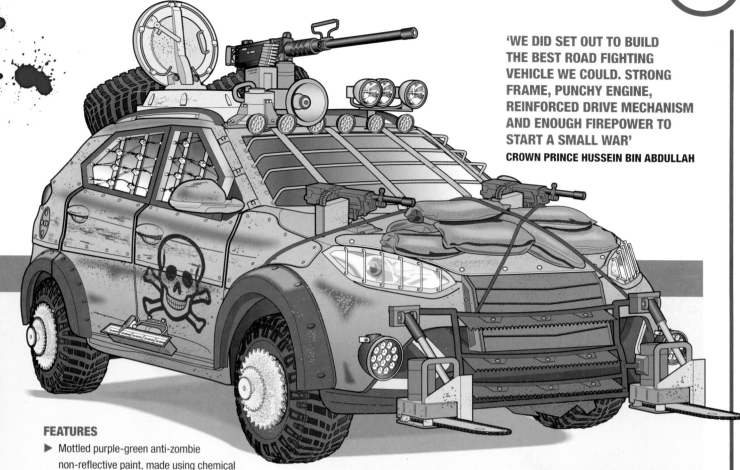

> 'WE DID SET OUT TO BUILD THE BEST ROAD FIGHTING VEHICLE WE COULD. STRONG FRAME, PUNCHY ENGINE, REINFORCED DRIVE MECHANISM AND ENOUGH FIREPOWER TO START A SMALL WAR'
> **CROWN PRINCE HUSSEIN BIN ABDULLAH**

FEATURES

- Mottled purple-green anti-zombie non-reflective paint, made using chemical compounds which repel the infected and create an inhospitable environment for the virus in any splattered blood.
- Reinforced darkened bulletproof windows with steel mesh protection. The zombies can't see you so there's always the option go quiet and release the dead scent from the under-vehicle decomposition unit causing any nearby zombies to lose interest.
- External storage racks for two full-sized spares wheels. Tyres are special issue Bridgestone Turanza Z001s.
- Four door access plus roof hatch and rear door emergency exit – ideally configured for rapid exit and entry when out foraging.
- On-board firework, smoke bomb and grenade launching unit, controlled from a central defensive systems array on the dashboard
- Light-weight B4 grade ballistic body armour around main body and doors.

- Roof mounted M60z firing head – smashing low velocity rounds which are also effective against bandits.
- Twin experimental Negev anti-zombie machine guns, firing experimental ghoul-busting dum dum bullets. Both guns are fed from an under-bonnet ammunition box.
- A network of 22 perimeter defence sensors around the vehicle which detect both movement and heat, feeding data back to the central defensive array on the dashboard. Vehicle also includes detachable sensors to establish a perimeter sensor network, for example during periods of sleep.
- Next generation Zombie Whistle Unit which generates noise at an ultrasonic level and is said to repel the dead and newly infected.
- Quad-batteries array on-board with a re-charging handle in the rear of the vehicle. An 'eternity' T100 start-up system ensures a minimal charge.

- Fully equipped Bug-Out Boot including a 5 gallon fresh water tank plus 5 internal lockable and 2 hidden compartments. Plus additional door storage unit for 10 military ready-to-eat meals.
- Secure on-board storage for two AK-47zs plus a ceiling holster for shotgun. A concealed handgun holster is under the steering column.
- Two horde clearer chainsaws at the front of the vehicle which move side to side to clear masses of the dead. These saws are retractable during off-road driving. Fully wrapped bull bars and an interior protective screen covering the engine.
- Communications array including a set of 5 2-way short-range 'walkie-talkie' units with encryption and military-grade location units. Plus a dashboard mounted CB system and a navigation suite with sealed unit and downloaded maps.

MOTORISED TRANSPORT

FUEL FOR SURVIVORS

With the right vehicle choice and the right maintenance regime, you should confidently be able to keep your vehicle 'on the road' and enjoy many years of happy, post-zombie apocalypse motoring. However, the biggest question on most survivalist agendas is about fuel – be it petrol or diesel. Will motoring survivalists face dry tanks within weeks or simply a small price hike at local 'end of the world' fuel outlets? Also, what about other forms of power? Living in the UK, we get enough sun rays per day to power a small matchbox car using solar energy. There are other options – hydrogen fuel cells, steam, coal, even utilising zombie power – but for most of us, it's going to be a Mad Max-like fuel grab. So where to nab that precious transport nectar?

HOW MUCH PETROL/DIESEL IS THERE IN THE UK?

The truth is no one really knows the answer else they just got too bored trying to work it out so here are some factors to consider:

▶ The UK national demand for road fuels is around 45 million litres of petrol per day, with around 1 billion litres in 'circulation' at any one time. The demand for diesel is around 77 million litres.

▶ There are around 8,500 petrol stations in the UK, virtually all of them with underground storage tanks. Most of them also serve a delightful range of snacks and hot drinks.

▶ At any one time, there are thought to be 10–20 fuel tankers dotted around the UK coast.

▶ THE FUEL LANDSCAPE

In consultation with experts – and we mean real experts – the Ministry of Zombies has put together the following graphic to illustrate the very real fuel challenges every survivor will face. However, you'll see that there are surprising sources of fuel as well – sites perhaps other looters and foragers will miss.

1 REFINERY COMPLEX

A good location to forage for fuel and other supplies in the early days but after a few months expect the site to have been taken over by an ambitious warlord. Only the biggest groups will have the resources to get a plant running and they may also start selling off fuel from any on-site storage tanks.

2 PETROL STATIONS

An obvious location which will become a hotbed of looting from day one – with the on-site shop being a clear target for supplies. Depending on the speed of the crisis, some stations will already be dry, with queues of empty and abandoned vehicles blocking the way.

3 FACTORIES AND DEPOTS

Many industrial and distribution sites have on-site fuel storage facilities. Post offices and anyone operating a delivery network are likely to provide particularly rich pickings for fuel foraging as well as good sites for spares and extras. Many of these sites will be overlooked during the initial fuel panic so get in early and grab what you can.

4 AIRPORTS

Every zombie survivalist knows to stay away from airports in the opening weeks of the crisis but as time goes on, they can provide useful sources of fuel supplies. Whilst aviation fuel is largely useless apart from use in a car-mounted flame thrower, it's the network of car parks which could provide the best areas for foraging.

5 CENTRES OF AUTHORITY

Remember, only forage from any emergency sites if you are sure that they are abandoned. Be sure that you don't interrupt any vital work against the zombies. However, if you do find any police, fire stations or other government sites, it's well worth a look around.

6 CAR SHOWROOMS AND GARAGES

Useful if you fancy grabbing a new vehicle for the apocalypse. Fuel storage on site is not typically very significant but there is usually a tank somewhere and any used cars outside would be worth checking out. Garages are likely to provide a similar haul in terms of fuel but are perfect locations for spares and consumables.

7 HOME SUPPLIES

Most homes will yield little in the way of fuel supplies bar the family car on the drive. If you happen to stumble on a well-prepared zombie prepper then you can expect them to be ready for any would-be looters. It may be possible to trade with them for fuel.

8 OTHER VEHICLES

Trawling the streets, looking for untouched cars will become a staple activity for many survivors hunting for fuel. It's important that you get your siphoning kit and skills ready to go and it's worth stocking up on some decent jerry cans to support your activities. You can expect fuel from cars in the street to become scarce very quickly.

▶ The immediate days after the breakdown of civilisation will see many of these locations looted, plundered and even burnt, particularly in urban areas. Remember the queues during recent strikes? – Quadruple that and throw in several hundred ravenous zombies.

▶ Official sources calculate that there are just over 35 million vehicles on our roads – referred to by vehicle geeks as the 'national vehicular stock'. In rough numbers, that's 30 million cars, 1.5 million motorcycles, 3.5 million vans, 350,000 HGVs, 170,000 buses/coaches and Grandad's pristine Rover 25. That's a lot of wheels. So, if you have the kit, there is plenty of fuel out there in tanks but it won't last forever.

▶ The whole fuel system is supported by a nationwide network of pipelines which move millions of tonnes of fuel around the UK, with road and rail transport being responsible for movement to end locations.

▶ A majority of the UK's fuel comes from 5–6 major refining locations across the country. Many of these sites have been established since the 1950s and are sprawling industrial complexes, often located on the coast to facilitate the transfer of tanker-transported crude oil. Importantly, each of these sites includes large storage terminals, mostly commonly recognised by the giant white cylinders which can be seen from miles around.

So what does it all mean? It means things are going to get frosty around any type of fuel. If you are a serious zombie prepper you can experiment with alternative power sources such as ethanol but, for most, this makes it even more important that you factor in fuel security into your Bug-Out Plans. There is plenty of information out there on other power options such as steam and even nuclear energy but, for the moment, you have to accept we live in a fossil fuel world.

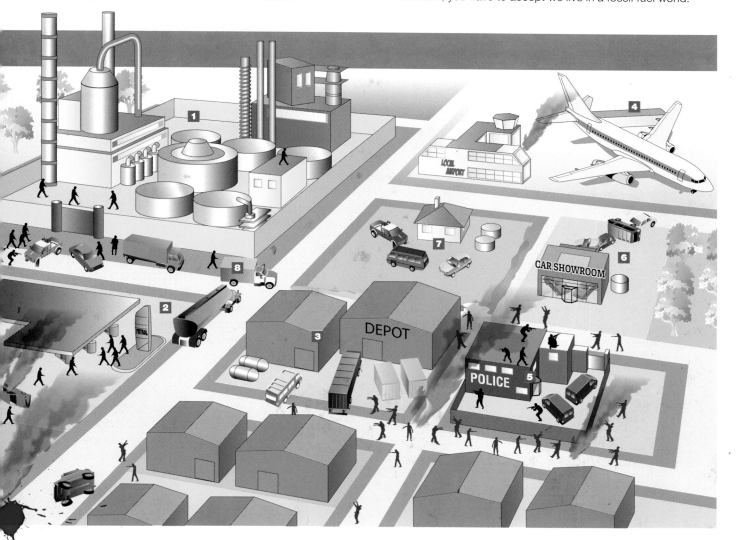

MOTORISED TRANSPORT

THE POST-APOCALYPTIC GARAGE

Whatever your Bug-Out Vehicle of choice, you will need a secure and well-equipped base from which to operate and maintain it. If you're planning on a long-range Bug-Out journey then it could be as simple as a location to keep your vehicle safe until it's needed. For example, you'll want to ensure it's safe from any prying eyes before the dead rise and that opportunistic bandits can't help themselves to it once the chaos begins. Equally, if you are planning to use your fortified home as a base

from which to forage and expand – then you'll need a secure workshop, fully equipped with spares, fuel and everything necessary to keep you on the road. Don't underestimate the challenge of building this vital workspace; it's just as important as your vehicle. In the new world, there won't be organised garages or the RAC. You might find some useful stores from which to forage supplies but in terms of maintenance and keeping mobile – you'll be on your own.

▶ END OF THE WORLD GARAGE

A fortified garage area is essential to keep you on the road after the end of the world. Like many survival projects, you can start small, for example by re-enforcing the front doors and meshing the windows. Create a plan for any work and make a rule to spend at least a day every week in your garage, either working on your vehicle, studying survival manuals or brushing up your mechanical skills. Ideally, the workshop should be within easy reach of your home complex or at least have a 'secure' route to your vehicle and supplies. The End of the World Garage in this case study in based on a real-life survivor example in Birmingham. The plans show the

core elements of the workshop but in reality, the owner has gone to significant lengths to ensure the site looks more like an abandoned lock up than a fully equipped workshop. For example, she secured a burnt-out wreck from a breakers yard which now sits on the drive. The roof and steel fence is largely covered by ivy, with a spoilt sofa blocking the door. At first glance, any would-be looters would just assume that it is some crumbling old building. 'No one outside the immediate family knows what I've built here,' she explains. 'Every bit has been smuggled in, mostly at night. Advertise your end of the world garage and it will be the first thing to go once the riots start.'

 LEGAL ADVICE

THERE ARE ALL TYPES OF HEALTH AND SAFETY CONCERNS AROUND THE STORAGE OF FUEL. AS A GENERAL GUIDELINE, PETROL IN A PURPOSE-BUILT SEALED CONTAINER SUCH AS A JERRY CAN WILL LAST 3–6 MONTHS BUT IF YOU ADD FUEL STABILISER, YOU CAN ADD ANOTHER 2–3 MONTHS ON TOP OF THIS. DIESEL FUEL CAN BE STORED FOR AROUND A YEAR WITH LITTLE DEGRADATION BUT IF YOU GET THE RIGHT CONDITIONS, IT CAN LAST A LOT LONGER.

1 LOCATION IS KEY
You must have easy access from your fortified home – the last thing you want is to be cut off from your vehicles in an emergency.

2 THE MAIN DOOR
If you have an old-fashioned up and over garage door, make it the first thing that you change. These older doors cave in with the least bit of pressure. Replace it with reinforced steel rollers or similar.

3 SURVIVAL LIBRARY
Keep a stock of survival books, including a Haynes manual of your particular vehicle. There will be long periods of inactivity during the crisis so use this time to top up your know-how.

4 TRAINING CERTIFICATES
Proudly display your mechanic and engineering qualifications. Track your achievements and learn everything you can about maintaining your vehicle.

5 EXTERIOR DEFENCES
A 2 metre reinforced steel fence is ideal but can stick out in an urban landscape. Razor wire can have much the same effect. A secure outside space is important so use items such as burnout cars or other debris to conceal your fortifications. If fencing is going to be too obvious then just go for fortified doors.

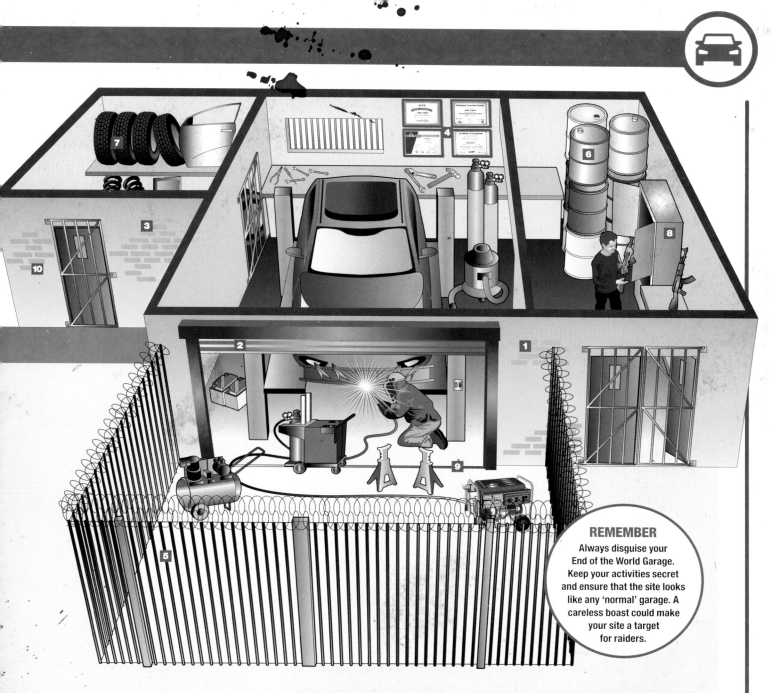

REMEMBER
Always disguise your
End of the World Garage.
Keep your activities secret
and ensure that the site looks
like any 'normal' garage. A
careless boast could make
your site a target
for raiders.

6 FUEL STORAGE
Ensure that you have a suitable and safe
fuel storage area. Remember to date any
fuels so you can rotate your stocks.

7 SPARES AND STORAGE
Maintain an ample supply of spare parts
and consumables. Check vehicle breaker
yards for extra parts but order other parts
such as batteries new.

8 TOOL CABINET
Maintain your stock and tools to ensure you
can maintain your vehicle and home.

9 SOUND AND LIGHT PROOFING
This can be an expensive alteration
but getting your location sound and
light proofed will ensure that you can
operate safely at all times whilst still
'running dark' to the outside world.
No other survivors will be aware of
any work you are doing inside and,
importantly, your constant banging
or Little Mix compilation won't attract
the unwelcome attention of the
walking dead.

10 A SECURE BOLTHOLE
Many zombie survival planners
build concealed boltholes within
their structures. This could be a
hidden cupboard or trapdoor to a
small fortified space you can hide
in if the need arises. Ensure you have
some basic supplies and water inside.
If raiders or zombies get in and you
can't defeat them, hiding could be
your only option to survive.

MOTORCYCLE OPTIONS

'Two wheels good, four wheels bad' is not something author George Orwell said but, had he known his motorbikes and some elements of basic zombie survival, he might well have.

Two wheeled and smaller vehicles such as quad bikes and dune buggies have some real advantages over larger options as they can weave through a landscape littered with broken vehicles and obstructions. They also have superb fuel economy – some specialist survival machines boast over 100 miles to the gallon.

There's plenty of choice out there. Obviously, budget is going to be a consideration – after all, not everyone has £25,000 for a custom-built American zombie apocalypse chopper. Could you make the same impact on raiders riding a jazzed-up Honda 50 moped complete with practical front shopping basket? Maybe not.

KNOW YOUR MACHINE

Checking your motorbike over is even more important than ever. Any breakdown in zombie land could prove fatal so remember all the basics – fuel, tyres, etc. Have a light-weight Bug-Out Bag on your vehicle at all times, even if it's stuffed in the bottom of a pannier. Importantly, have a good understanding of your machine's ability – if it's a smart road cruiser don't get caught trying to ride over a major obstruction – know, for example, your ground clearance levels.

Most experts predict that poor training and poor knowledge of their bike will get more riders killed during a zombie outbreak than anything else.

OPTION 1
MINI-BIKES

Not the children's models, the fully working versions often used by people dropping off hire cars. Some models can fold and fit in the back of a car. Fast enough to get you out of trouble when required and yet small enough to be part of an on-board Bug-Out Kit on a larger vehicle. The low-profile makes the rider hard to spot but range is limited, particularly on the electric versions. Not great stability wise and suffers from naturally low ground clearance. The petrol versions tend to be noisy and attract the zombies but are better performers speed-wise. It might be worth snagging a couple and keeping them in the back of your Bug-Out Garage.

 Poor. The lower you are, the more likely you are to get grabbed. Might be a useful addition if you have ample storage space on your vehicle. But still, only use in real emergencies.

OPTION 2
MOPEDS/SCOOTERS

From mods to grannies, mopeds and scooters are everywhere so availability of these machines is excellent. Basic models are easy to maintain and there are plenty of spare parts out there. 50cc mopeds tend to have a maximum speed of around 40 mph but some larger-engine scooters are faster. A low centre of gravity increases your chances of a crash on obstructed roads. Plus, you will look a bit of an old fart given the choice of other vehicles available, unless you manage to pick up a Quadrophenia-type 250cc super-scooter – more likely you'll end up on a former pizza-delivery moped struggling up hills, weighed down with foraged supplies.

 Good. A basic moped could be a useful back-up option but it's not for a primary vehicle. If you have the budget, it's worth nabbing a cheap second-hand moped and keeping safe.

OPTION 3
ROAD CRUISER

Powerful and extremely quick, these machines are built for performance and speed. To be fair, it's a broad category covering everything from street-legal racing machines to long-distance cruisers, the latter of which can be a useful long-range Bug-Out options, particularly machines such as the Honda Gold Wing series and many of the BMW hybrid cruisers. Generally very good fuel economy and outstanding reliability. The racing machines are great on perfect roads but post-zombie apocalypse roads won't be perfect. They also have 'steal me' written all over it. New machines require specialist technical maintenance and tools.

 Racing machines are not ideal as the road conditions won't suit your sparkling new mean machine. Hybrid road cruisers with greater off-road capability are a better choice.

KNOW YOURSELF

Expert riders always say 'ride within your capabilities'. Sensible advice for normal times but in the chaos of the apocalypse, even more important. Even a minor accident could get you eaten. Training is key – get as much riding training as you can before the dead rise.

LOOKING AHEAD

Target or destination fixation can tempt even experienced riders to focus in the distance when they should be focusing on the road in front. Keep your attention on the road ahead and on any obstructions – that awkwardly parked car or group of desperate survivors hastily putting together an ambush.

PRACTICE DEFENSIVE RIDING

The danger of hostile human drivers is ever-present. Some will see you as a tempting prospect, hoping to knock you off then help themselves to whatever loot you are carrying. Learn how to ride defensively. Use your manoeuvrability and speed.

OPTION 4
OFF-ROAD BIKES

Perfect for scrambling around roadblocks or across country, these hard-wearing machines are widely available, with many off-road scramblers coming stripped of any non-essential extras. Ensure that you get a reasonable engine size to ensure you have the power and you'll have an excellent machine for the wasteland, capable of clearing most obstacles. The main downside is the noise, with many competition machines barely meeting legal standards so ensure that you check any bike before you buy it as part of your Bug- Out plans. There's a healthy used vehicle market and with common models, spares shouldn't be an issue.

 Very Good. A great short-range Bug-Out vehicle or for foraging. Just get plenty of riding practice before the dead arrive.

OPTION 5
TRIKES

Like off-road bikes, trikes are a great short-range Bug-Out Vehicle and are also good for foraging. Just get plenty of riding practice in before the dead arrive. It's worth fitting some light panniers as storage options aren't great. At reasonable speeds, stability and manoeuvrability tends to be good but riders need to be familiar with trikes, as there are important differences between 3-wheelers and cars or other motorcycles, particularly the cornering and stability. Advantages are that you can carry passengers and loot. The downsides are that you lack protective cover and the off-road capability of a decent 2-wheeler.

 Good. You'll be a king of the road but will lose the benefits of a 2-wheeled motorcycle and pick up some of the drawbacks of a larger car-like vehicle.

OPTION 6
ATV/QUADS

The stability of a car with the agility of a bike – what's not to love? Good speed and great off-road capability, and with useful people and load carrying options. This broad range of vehicles is a staple feature at most survivalist conventions, from purpose-built 'end of the world' quads to 6-wheel all-terrain amphibious 'ducks'. On most vehicles, the rider is exposed and quad bikes are often more powerful than new riders realise, so it's worth getting some practice in before the apocalypse. Stick to the better known and most common models then adapt from there. Specialist zombie machines tend to be expensive and have to be imported.

 Excellent. As a primary or back-up vehicle, a solid and practical choice for the apocalypse. Any good Honda, Yamaha or Bombardier model should be a sound platform to build on.

MOTORCYCLE OPTIONS

ZOMBIES AND MOTORCYCLES

There are many dangers out there for motorcyclists in the zombie wasteland. One is that a shambling zombie, attracted by either the noise or movement of your bike, strays into your path. Zombie in the road – bash – you're on the ground getting feasted upon by the rest of the horde. The second danger is grabbers. Be it from the ground or car window, this is a risk for any rider. As one zombie survival rider put it: 'I knew a rider who was caught by a zombie from a car window. The thing stuck its hand out and just held on. The rider carried on and the arm just tore off. The thing kept clawing and in the end the guy panicked and rode into a parked car.'

If you are planning to use a motorcycle as part of your survival plans beyond just scrambling around on a stripped down off-roader, then you need a powerful, heavy-weight machine, with a low centre of gravity and enough on-board storage to carry at least 48 hours of supplies. There are specialist machines available on the market – the Liberty Freedom Wasteland Chopper is one such bike – but they can be beyond the budget of many preppers. Remember that it's quite possible to convert a 'standard' machine by making some alterations. Look through the features on the Liberty Freedom Chopper for some ideas.

▶ LIBERTY 'FREEDOM' WASTELAND CHOPPER

Fantastic fuel economy, cooler than a freezer at Iceland and nothing says 'bad ass' like the Liberty 'Freedom' Wasteland Chopper – being able to scare opponents could just help you stay alive in zombie town. But this no normal motorcycle, the Freedom Chopper was created by a team of specialist mechanics and zombie survival experts and boasts a host of features to help you rule the wasteland. Available in the 'standard' tourer version, there is also a massive range of extras, such as supplementary fuel storage, crossbow holders and smart-code start up. The company slogan is 'No one messes with a Freedom Chopper.'

'THE TENNESSEE MOTORCYCLE COMPANY SET OUT TO BUILD THE BEST APOCALYPSE-READY MOTORCYCLE WE COULD. WE WANTED TO BUILD THE KIND OF BIKE THAT WOULD GET A SURVIVOR AND PARTNER TO THEIR BUG-OUT LOCATION AT THE END OF THE WORLD'
TENNESSEE MOTORCYCLE COMPANY

THE LIBERTY 'FREEDOM' WASTELAND CHOPPER
Tennessee Motorcycle Company, 400 units sold worldwide in 2017

PURPOSE
The ultimate wasteland tourer. See the world solo or with a dream partner and look bad enough to put any opponents off.

TECHNICAL SPECIFICATIONS
Ultima 2.0 dual-fuel engine, liquid cooled. 6-speed transmission with a monocoque aluminium frame. Front suspension Marzocchi 50 mm pressurised forks in hard anodised aluminium. Rear fully adjustable Sachs unit. Front brakes 2,340 mm semi-floating zombie-shielded discs. Rear brakes single 250 mm sealed disc. Front tyre 120/70 ZombieR Pirelli Devil. Rear tyre 200/55 ZombieR Pirelli Demon.

ARMAMENTS
None as standard but optional fittings for handguns, grenade pouches, semi-automatics and crossbow holder. As one UK owner explained – 'This is a chopper screaming to be "tooled up"'.•

CREW
1 plus 1 pillion. Survival panniers are included as standard.

BUDGET
The standard tourer version starts at £25,000. There are custom build options; a brochure is available on request. Options include booster panniers, shotgun pouch and a cleverly shaped extra drinking water tank.

RANGE
300 miles on a standard configuration tank. With the supplementary fuel reserve, can manage 400–500 miles. The multi-fuel engine boasts up to 80 miles to the gallon.

USAGE GUIDELINES
This purpose-built zombie apocalypse chopper is superb wasteland cruiser, with more than enough anti-ghoul features to see you through the outbreak. Ideal as an urban raider for exploring or foraging and with its supplementary fuel tank, can also serve as longer-range Bug-Out Vehicle. Keep out of sight for the first month or so, and then emerge from the garage, complete with your crossbow and survival poncho.

'THE END OF CIVILISATION DOESN'T HAVE TO MEAN THE END OF THE FUN'

LIBERTY CHOPPER
ADVERTISING SLOGAN

FEATURES

▶ Military grade – uses military-grade parts across the engine including self-cleaning cooling fans and anti-block feed pipes and pumps – basically, zombie guts and gunk aren't going to stop the Wasteland Chopper.

▶ Modern metals – wide use of aluminium across the machine so it so only weighs 250 lbs unladen. Light enough to be controllable but with enough mass to punch through zombie hordes if required. Open optional front screen is available.

▶ Survival Panniers – lockable stowage compartment with in-built water and fuel filtration units, room for two 48 hour Bug-Out Bags and an armoured ammunition box. Hidden unit underneath to keep an emergency key.

▶ On-board Weapon Holsters – optional fitting for 'easy access' shotgun storage unit with optional parts to fit weapons such as the Kel-Tec-KSG or longer weapons such as the Remington Model 887. A clever rear catch is designed to hold either a bow or crossbow. There is also additional concealed storage for a small handgun.

▶ Additional Motorcycle Backpack – a hardwearing reinforced canvas sack which fits to the rear of the bike and can be used to store sheeting, tents or other Bug-Out Supplies.

▶ Good ground clearance – a small compromise in the chopper design has lead to slightly shorter front forks and a larger than normal front-wheel to ensure the machine has suitable ground clearance to traverse the wasteland.

▶ Ultima Engine – powerful enough to get you out of any trouble but light enough to give the chopper near-perfect balance – this motor is perfectly suited to the ravages of the wasteland, with a robust filtration system, plus it will run on just about anything.

▶ ZombieR Pirelli Tyres – these bad boys are made for the end times, almost impossible to puncture, military-grade rubberised compound and unique anti-zombie gunk tread.

▶ Gunk proof brake unit – both the front semi-floating discs and the rear single-disc brakes operate as sealed units.

ADVICE ON HELMETS

Protecting your melon when riding or driving any open vehicle during a zombie outbreak is as important as it is now, if not more so. Riders have heard the arguments before:

▶ A quality crash helmet can seriously reduce the risk of head injury and death during an accident

▶ A helmet will also protect you against zombie bites – 21% of zombie bites are to the head and neck area.

▶ It will also protect you from small projectiles hurled by opportunistic survivors looking for easy loot.

> **IMPORTANT**
> Always wear a helmet when riding a motorcycle. The benefits far outweigh the disadvantages.

51

POST-APOCALYPTIC DRIVING

This section outlines the skills you need to develop to survive not only Z-Day but also the growing chaos and violence of the post-apocalyptic world it leaves behind. After all, zombies aren't the only menace you're going to face out there on the roads.

Whatever your vehicle, it is important that you quickly adapt to driving or riding in a post-apocalyptic landscape. A couple of obvious examples will be dealing with various obstructions that will increasingly dominate our roads or the thousands of zombies milling around. However, also consider the new dangers of night-driving on unlit roads and the ever-present threat of human opponents – bandits or even just desperate survivors looking to run you off the road and help themselves to your kit. Training to drive in true zombie apocalypse conditions is impossible. You can, for example, complete various off-road and defensive driving courses and there is no doubt that these will help but nothing can prepare you for the full horror of an M25 littered with burning lorries, over-turned cars, trapped survivors and the walking dead scouring the landscape for those left alive. This section is all about surviving on post-apocalyptic roads and will provide you with a survival framework including facts, considerations and some basic manoeuvres. Nothing can replace real-life practice though so get as much training as you can and practice some of these techniques in controlled conditions.

POST-APOCALYPTIC DRIVING
DRIVER AWARENESS

Working with the Department for Transport, the Ministry of Zombies has created a training framework for driving awareness in conditions affected by a major zombie outbreak. It is hoped that from 2020, elements from this syllabus will be included in the UK's driving theory test, with a focus on zombie hazard perception. In the practical test there will be added elements such as controlling a vehicle with a 'screen blocker', where a zombie is clutching onto the windscreen wipers blocking the view – the manoeuvre is similar to an emergency stop.

> * THE DEPARTMENT FOR TRANSPORT REQUESTED THAT THE FOLLOWING DISCLAIMER BE MADE
> *The Department for Transport does not endorse Module 3 of the Zombie Apocalypse Driver Awareness programme. It is not an objective of this government department to turn leaner or experienced drivers into 'Mad Max-style road warriors'. It is therefore unlikely that 'pulling a j-turn' or 'clipping the dead' will included in the UK driving test any time in the near-future.*

MODULE 1
CONTEXT & ENVIRONMENT

This module involves drivers learning about the general features of post-apocalyptic driving including understanding threats, getting the right driver mentality for the conditions and vehicle preparation.

MODULE 2
ZOMBIE AWARENESS

This module looks at the zombie threat to vehicular transport and drivers, including not only defensive driving techniques but also tried and trusted manoeuvres to deal with the zombie menace.

MODULE 3
HOSTILE HUMANS *

This controversial module focuses on the human impact of the zombie apocalypse. It considers the 'dark skills' required to survive on post-zombie apocalypse streets dominated by desperate survivors and bandits.

► CREATE A BUG-OUT ZONE

Consider your secure location in the context of your 'Bug-Out Zone' – that is the immediate area around your home and how it supports your survival and Bug-Out Plans. For example, you'll certainly need a good map, marking Bug-Out Routes and other secure locations for use in emergencies. This diagram shows the ideal – most preppers can't afford to have a fully-equipped alternative Bug-Out Vehicle in a fortified lock up but do carefully assess your current location. The principles apply whether you live in a detached or terraced home, or even an apartment.

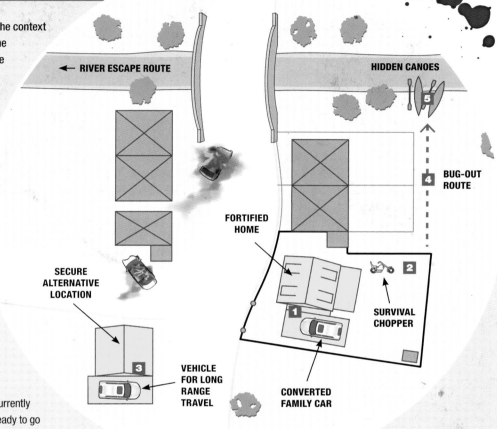

RIVER ESCAPE ROUTE

HIDDEN CANOES

BUG-OUT ROUTE

FORTIFIED HOME

SECURE ALTERNATIVE LOCATION

SURVIVAL CHOPPER

VEHICLE FOR LONG RANGE TRAVEL

CONVERTED FAMILY CAR

1 Your primary Bug-Out Vehicle currently locked in a secure garage but ready to go complete with fuel and Bug-Out Supplies. This is the vehicle that hopefully sees you through the end of the world. You've prepared it, looked after it and now it's ready to face the zombie hordes.

2 There's a survival chopper motorcycle hidden in the garden. It's only a short-range machine but it's intended for foraging around the local area. If the roads are blocked or you don't want to risk your primary vehicle, this is what you use to survey the ruins of civilisation.

3 Your secondary Bug-Out Vehicle is nearby. In this case, it's an old diesel you've maintained and restored, ideal for longer-range journeys. It's stored in the house of a neighbour who lives abroad. People rarely visit the house and only you and your immediate party know about it. Keep it that way!

4 A concealed Bug-Out Route through the nearby woods to the river. It's not a main Bug-Out Route. It's not marked on any of your maps, which could be stolen. This is your emergency path down to the riverside. If zombies or bandits overrun the street and if the roads are completely blocked, this will be your lifeline.

5 Hidden by the river, under a shrub bush, are a couple of canoes, complete with waterproof Bug-Out Bags. You can't see them from the river or the roadside. These waterborne Bug-Out Vehicles are your insurance policy. If things get toasty, you'll head towards these canoes and silently paddle away from the danger.

'DON'T BECOME OBSESSED WITH CREATING THE PERFECT BUG-OUT PLAN. NOT EVERYONE WILL HAVE THE BUDGET FOR MULTIPLE LAYERS OF ESCAPE VEHICLE. START SIMPLE AND LOOK FOR COST-EFFECTIVE AND PRACTICAL OPTIONS. GET YOUR PRIMARY AND SECONDARY VEHICLE SORTED. AFTER THAT, DEVELOP YOUR SYSTEM AS YOU DEVELOP YOUR SKILLS OR HAVE THE BUDGET TO DO SO'
JULIAN HENDRY,
SKILLS FOR THE END OF THE WORLD

POST-APOCALYPTIC DRIVING

CONTEXT AND ENVIRONMENT

If you've done your UK car or motorcycle driving test then you will often have heard fellow drivers say things like, 'It's different on the test, it's not like real life' and, 'You really start learning once you've passed'. This is true enough and it's the same for the driving conditions after a major zombie outbreak. Being aware of your environment and understanding your vehicle will be vital skills needed to keep you and your group alive.

THREATS ON THE ROAD AFTER Z-DAY

The chart below should guide your transport plans for the apocalypse. For example, it's clear that crashes and collisions kill as many drivers as the zombies do. Also, the figures show the very real threat of human action such as theft and banditry. It's essential that you understand just how much the driving landscape has changed. Remember, these figures relate to the opening few weeks of an outbreak. None of these incidents lasted longer than a month and after this period the number of vehicle breakdowns will increase.

THE C.R.A.Z. SYSTEM

For longer-term predictions, the Ministry of Zombies uses the following **C.R.A.Z** system.

30%	**C**ollision
20%	**R**oad War
30%	**A**uto-breakdown
20%	**Z**ombie Incident

The C.R.A.Z tool is used in all UK and European Union zombie defence planning and offers an aggregated prediction model which estimates 'transportation' casualties during an ongoing zombie apocalypse. So, what it's saying is that of course you need to learn about zombies but collisions, breakdowns and road war incidents will take out far more drivers than the walking dead. This fact has been used to ensure that any military and emergency personnel are as confident in their vehicle and their driving skills as they are at running down the walking dead.

POST-APOCALYPTIC DRIVING DRIVER DEATHS

Before learning how to do a J-turn in your snazzy new Bug-Out Vehicle, it's worth looking at exactly how the road users who died in previous zombie outbreaks met their end. The following chart is made up of data from the 3 major zombie outbreaks, all of which lasted more than 3 weeks, so it's the best information we have.

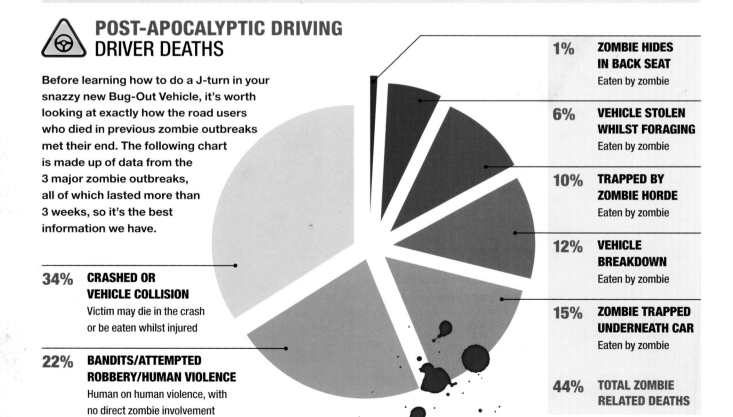

1% ZOMBIE HIDES IN BACK SEAT
Eaten by zombie

6% VEHICLE STOLEN WHILST FORAGING
Eaten by zombie

10% TRAPPED BY ZOMBIE HORDE
Eaten by zombie

12% VEHICLE BREAKDOWN
Eaten by zombie

15% ZOMBIE TRAPPED UNDERNEATH CAR
Eaten by zombie

44% TOTAL ZOMBIE RELATED DEATHS

34% CRASHED OR VEHICLE COLLISION
Victim may die in the crash or be eaten whilst injured

22% BANDITS/ATTEMPTED ROBBERY/HUMAN VIOLENCE
Human on human violence, with no direct zombie involvement

SOURCE: MINISTRY OF ZOMBIES OFFICE OF STATISTICS, BASED ON OUTBREAKS IN PERU 1984, THAILAND 2001 AND ITALY 2004.

► POST-APOCALYPTIC ROAD CONDITIONS

1 BLOCKS, JAMS AND ROADBLOCKS

By now you should be aware that the arrival of the zombies will see a mindless rush onto our roads as the crowds try to use their poorly maintained people carriers to flee the dead. Combine this with abandoned roadblocks and broken down vehicles and many carriageways will be impassable to most vehicles. You will need to start making a map early on. Some routes will be clear; some will be mangled no-go areas dominated by horrific uncleared crashes and clustered zombie populations.

2 DETERIORATING ROAD CONDITIONS

It is unlikely that the local council will continue filling in potholes after the end of the world and, as the seasons pass, expect things to get much more challenging on the UK's roads. You'll be seeing more collapsed manhole covers, deep suspension-busting potholes and larger sinkholes. This will all be in addition to the everyday hazards of general debris and road wreckage. If you are planning on using a snazzy mid-life crisis sports car as your post-apocalyptic vehicle, then you may want to reconsider that 6 mm ground clearance at the front.

3 FLOODS

Water deserves a special mention here in the UK and Ireland. Expect to encounter far more floods than normal as rivers burst their banks and fight back to their natural courses and leaks go unfixed. Remember, it's not as simple as driving through a shallow puddle. Never drive through water unless you know the maximum depths you will be facing. Also, hitting deep water at speed can be like crashing into a brick wall. Be cautious, plan your way around if necessary and avoid become a watery snack for any opportunistic ghouls.

4 TUNNELS, BRIDGES AND COLLAPSES

Worth a special mention as many are such crucial parts of our transport infrastructure. How long do you trust a bridge for? Months, years? What about a dark tunnel? The latter is to be avoided at all costs. If you've seen any zombie movies then you will know that driving into a long dark tunnel rarely ends well. Over time, the danger of the undead will be replaced by collapses as maintenance schedules are abandoned and burning wrecks are left to do their damage. Our bridges may fair better — at least any danger should be more visible — but still approach with caution. As the years go by, expect structural faults to develop and for them to eventually become too dangerous to use.

'THE FISCAL BUDGET FOR ZOMBIE SURVIVAL ROAD PLANNING HAS INCREASED BY £200 MILLION SINCE THE 2011 FOLKESTONE OUTBREAK. THAT'S DESPITE AN OVERALL REDUCTION IN THE BUDGET OF £250 MILLION SINCE THE AUSTERITY CUTS DURING FISCAL YEAR 2008–9 AND A 50% CUT IN ZOMBIE-PROOFING GRANTS'
THE UK HIGHWAYS AGENCY*

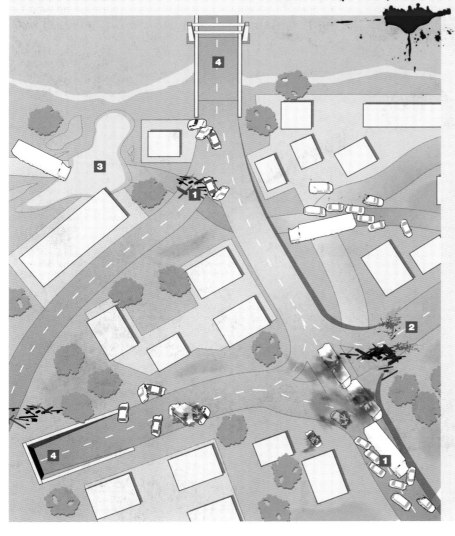

* A CONFUSING RESPONSE TO A FREEDOM OF INFORMATION REQUEST BY THE MINISTRY OF ZOMBIES IN APRIL 2017.

POST-APOCALYPTIC DRIVING

ZOMBIE AWARENESS

There are two general areas to consider – how to drive safely on roads dominated by the undead and then how you can safely use your vehicle to help humanity by reducing the number of dead on the roads. The first is the most important but the second one is far more interesting – who doesn't want to use their pimping post-apocalyptic vehicle to run zombies over?

First things first – this manual is about helping you prepare to get around in the wake of a zombie outbreak, and, for most, this will mean getting out there and enjoying our post-apocalyptic roadways. Secondly, although zombies don't drive (hopefully you already knew that), the millions of dead milling around will impact on your journey – whether you plan a short foraging trip or a major cross country relocation.

SURVIVOR OR ZOMBIE?

Everyone loves running down a zombie – it's a fact of life – but the activity is not without its dangers. Some survivors advocate avoiding it all together, others see it as a community-spirited and fun way to trim down their numbers. What is certain is that you need to be sure it's a zombie before you approach at ramming speed.

'CAUSING THE DEATH OF AN INFECTED INDIVIDUAL BY MEANS OF A VEHICLE IS BY NO MEANS CLEAR LEGALLY. ANY PRESIDING AUTHORITY WOULD NEED TO WEIGH THE DEGREE OF INFECTION OF THE VICTIM AGAINST THE VERY OBVIOUS BENEFIT OF WHACKING A FEW ZOMBIES'
GUIDO RAMOULDI, THE EUROPEAN COURT OF HUMAN RIGHTS

▶ HOW TO CONTROL A CAR SKIDDING ON ZOMBIES

Cars skid for many reasons – in normal times, the main cause is braking too hard in wet conditions. Post-apocalyptic conditions certainly contain this danger but to this we should add what is technically known as 'zombie road gunk'.

WHAT IS ZOMBIE ROAD GUNK?
With thousands of dead on the roads, material from crushed body parts, including intestine content and internal body organs, will combine to create a highly viscous sludgy mess known as zombie road gunk.

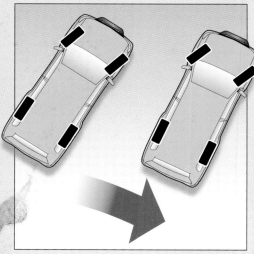

STEP 1
AVOIDANCE
Be aware of the road surface, particularly if you are running down groups of zombies. The threat will be higher in wet conditions for obvious reasons. Do not brake hard, slow down when hitting zombies and drive at an appropriate speed. This skill requires practice – it's about controlling your vehicle.

STEP 2
DON'T PANIC
If you feel your vehicle starting to slip, stay calm. Jamming your foot down on either the brake or the accelerator could see you ramming in to the nearest wall. First step is to gently ease up on the gas and attempt to regain control of the vehicle if possible. You may still be able to stop a total loss of control.

POST-APOCALYPTIC DRIVING
TIPS FOR CLIPPING THE DEAD

Safely 'clipping' zombies in the wasteland not only provides a useful service to the rest of humanity, but it can also be a very therapeutic way to spend an afternoon during the 'end times'. But you need to bash the zombies in a safe and efficient way. These simple rules should guarantee hours of carefree zombie crushing.

1 Ensure that your vehicle is prepared for the wasteland, including frontal protection and meshed windows. Remember, your vehicle should be in 'good working order'.

2 You should aim to 'clip' the zombie with the side of your vehicle unless it is purposely designed to run down and flatten the walking dead. Solder on some clipping wings with blades or spikes to increase the entertainment value of a hit.

3 Further enhance the fun and the drama by using games such as walking dead snooker. Be aware the zombies dressed in red become increasingly difficult to find so don't take risks just to get that stray ghoul.

4 Manage your speed carefully – you don't need masses of speed to be effective and it will only increase the risk of an accident. Don't become obsessed with hitting a particular zombie – there will be plenty out there for you. Sometimes, you'll just need to let it go.

5 Be patient and choose your targets carefully. You may be able to get higher points by identifying clusters of zombies. Be wary of hidden obstructions such as bollards or you could find yourself being clipped by the dead.

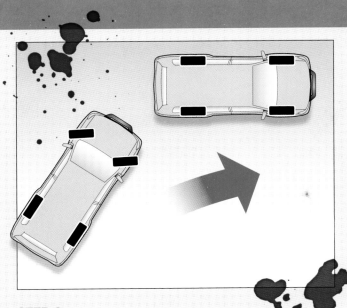

STEP 3
RECOVERING FROM A SKID

As the gas is eased, if the wheels skid to the right then gently steer in that direction. Use slight movements and the vehicle will begin to straighten up. (Reverse the steering direction as required for a skid to the left.) Again, these manoeuvres require a cool head and calm thinking, which is tough if you have passengers panicking on-board.

STEP 4
BACK TO NORMAL

As the vehicle straightens, gently level up the steering wheel to leave the car looking forward. You may want to bring the vehicle to a stop if it's safe to do so to give yourself a breather. Always complete a quick perimeter check once your vehicle has come to a halt. Don't let it play over in your mind – there will be time for that later on. Now, it's about survival.

POST-APOCALYPTIC DRIVING

HIDDEN DANGERS

A crowd of zombies hanging around on the corner of a deserted high street is just asking to be run down but drivers beware as crowds or even lone zombies could be hiding any number of obstructions such as bollards, large kerbs or even walls. They might look like a tempting target but if you're not sure, don't proceed. It is pointless incapacitating your vehicle, or worse, just to deal with a gang of rotting ghouls. The post-apocalyptic transport landscape will be a minefield of dangers, particularly on unexplored roads so ensure that you stay in 'survival mode' as you drive through the wasteland. This is why experts only recommend 2 hours of apocalypse driving before taking a break. Your attention needs to be on at all times and your focus sharp. If possible, switch with another team member using a rotation system.

THE ZIG-ZAG FLIP

The Zig-Zag Flip is a reckless manoeuvre so common that it's even got its own name and is typically mentioned on every post-zombie apocalypse driving course when discussing what not to do on the roads during a zombie apocalypse. It involves hapless and over-excited drivers veering across roads trying to hit particular zombies, only for them to lose control of their vehicle and see it flip over. The situation sounds unlikely but experience of outbreaks has shown that it is a leading cause of zombie–related road traffic accidents (ZRTAs). No one likes to let a zombie get away and this sometimes leads drivers to take inappropriate risks as they try to catch that 'old one with the funny hat' or the 'lanky hippy with the backpack'. Avoid becoming the next victim of the Zig-Zag Flip by always staying 'frosty' at the wheel – never let emotion take over.

▶ HOW TO MANAGE A SCREEN BLOCKER

Most drivers enjoy running down zombies – it's one of the few pleasures of the wasteland and, most of the time, you can also enjoy the satisfying crunch as the dead are directed underneath the vehicle. Job done – another of the undead hordes dealt with as a service to humanity. However, on occasions a zombie will flip upwards and land on your windscreen blocking your view. The creature can become entangled and leave you struggling to see the road ahead so you need to know how to deal with Screen Blockers.

ACCESSING YOUR VEHICLE

Many new cars are designed with front crumple zones and other features to protect people in any collision scenario. This makes sense for normal times but you should assess the front area of your vehicle to determine whether it is likely to direct zombies over or under. Many survivalists fit full steel bull bars or angled grills to ensure that they don't create a steady flow of the dead over the bonnet. Ensure that the front of your vehicle is fit for zombie bashing before you start.

STEP 1
MANAGING THE SHOCK

Picture this – you're driving along mashing zombies under the wheel when suddenly you hear a loud bang and the car goes dark. The initial shock of a zombie blocking your screen can be enough to cause an accident. Your first reaction will be to brake hard but it's important that you manage any shock before making your move.

POST-APOCALYPTIC DRIVING
UNWANTED PASSENGERS

A less exciting danger but one which will probably take down more survivors than any other zombie road hazard – in the course of driving around the wasteland, you are bound to pick up stray zombies that either grab onto or become hooked onto your vehicle.

Varieties of zombie such as Undercar Exhaust Grabbers could become caught underneath, only to emerge once you are safely parked in your secure compound. You may find limbless wonders still grabbing on to the boot after parking, ready to catch the unaware survivor. Remember, whenever you park your vehicle, listen for any groaning and complete a visual check before leaving. Don't let other survivors get caught by an oil-soaked ghoul you brought into a secure area.

WARNING!
THE MINISTRY OF ZOMBIES ADVISE CAUTION WHEN CHECKING

STEP 2
TAKING ACTION

Braking hard is useful as it will often send the zombie flying forward and clearing your windscreen but always check your mirrors first as, for example, if you are in a convoy, you could create a serious accident. Where possible, slow the vehicle without ramming on the brakes, bringing it to a controlled stop to avoid skidding.

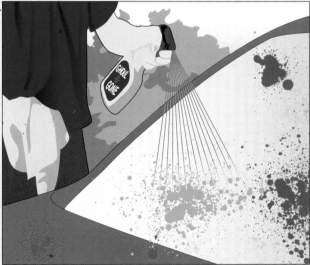

STEP 3
CLEARING UP

Once it's safe to do so, clear your windscreen of any zombie or body parts, being careful in case ghouls are present underneath the vehicle. Use a decent cleaner to clear off the gunk – water will often just leave you with a greasy mess of rotting body fluids.

POST-APOCALYPTIC DRIVING

HOSTILE HUMANS

You've read your zombie survival manual, you've got your base and transport sorted and you're cruising the wasteland in your ideal survival vehicle. Now for the bad news. There are plenty of not great folks out there who are going to want to take your stuff, your car and even your life. What you learnt from your driving instructor may help you reverse into a parking space at Tesco but it won't cover high-speed getaways or pulling an emergency J-turn.

AMBUSHES

Expect no end of variation and tricks as they become more desperate and in some cases more organised. An 'ambush' is any occasion when you're taken by surprise in your vehicle. Generally, experts recognise two main types:

▶ STATIC AMBUSH

This type involves you having to stop or go slowly through a 'kill zone'. Imagine armed gang organised ad-hoc roadblocks or check points at junctions or crossing points. Expect them to use deception, perhaps posing as soldiers or peaceful survivors. As law and order collapses, groups will spring up in some areas.

▶ ROLLING AMBUSH

This type happens on the move. For example, a vehicle might overtake with a gun firing off into the air. Their task is to distract you and get you to stop. Meanwhile, you'll be hemmed in from both behind and side by other supporting vehicles. Their objective is to take away your mobility. Once you stop, you'll be surrounded by armed assailants.

▶ HOW TO COMPLETE A J-TURN

You are bound to have seen a J-turn in various action movies – it's where the car reverses then pulls a complete 180 degree turn to keep driving in the same direction but without losing any speed. It's a hard manoeuvre to master but is invaluable if you need to reverse out of trouble in a hurry. A successful J-turn will enable you to make your escape and give you a head start over any intruders. Completing the move successfully in front of any bandits may be enough to convince them that you're not worth messing with.

STEP 1
REVERSE BACKWARDS

Scan your surroundings. You don't need lots of space but you do need to know you're not going to hit anything and can complete your spin. Throw the vehicle into reverse but keep looking forward. Pump the accelerator and get some speed up. It takes some practice but you should continue to look forward.

STEP 2
STEERING

Get one hand on the steering wheel at the 04.30 or 07.30 position depending on which way you are going spin and grab the gear shift with the other hand. Give the blocking bandits an icy stare and prepare to leave them gawping in admiration and, hopefully, some fear.

POST-APOCALYPTIC DRIVING
AVOIDING AN AMBUSH

The best ambush defence tactic is to avoid it in the first place. For the survival novice this can sound like a case of stating the bleedin' obvious but recognising some of the signs can give you that vital early mover advantage.

SPOT THE DANGER EARLY
Be aware of the signs, always scan ahead and be suspicious of anyone else on the road. You'll soon develop a sixth sense for these things. Know when to avoid locations or roads.

STOPPING IN THE 'KILL ZONE'
Whatever their objective, your opponents want to immobilise you in their prepared kill-zone so if at all possible avoid this. Use manoeuvres such as the J-turn to buy you a fighting chance at making an escape.

USE CAR AND BODY ARMOUR
If your attackers are primarily interested in your loot, they may chance a few rounds into your vehicle so where possible use car armour and body armour – these could be a life-saver.

COUNTERING AN AMBUSH
Experienced drivers will tell you that there isn't a text book way to get out of an ambush. Every situation is different and you need to fall back on an arsenal of skills and techniques. Always expect a secondary ambush so your priority is to get out of the kill zone as quickly as possible.

You'll often hear experienced zombie fighters say that they just 'don't like a particular set up' and move on. Learn to trust your gut even if it means missing out on some valuable loot.

STEP 3
GAS OFF, STEERING OVER
Let up on the gas and the weight of the vehicle will shift towards the rear. At the same time, yank the wheel as sharply as you can to induce the vehicle into a 180 degree spin. At this point, any survivors in your vehicle will be thrown from side to side so don't forget to tell them what you're planning. It's worth having a code phrase you can shout so as not to tip off any bad guys. Something simple such as 'Momma likes the spice!'

STEP 4
MAKING YOUR ESCAPE
Once your vehicle is turning and once it hits 90 degrees, yank the steering wheel back into an upright position. If you get your timing right, you should be facing the other way with little reduction in speed and be able to make good your escape, leaving the breathless bandits with the choice to either pursue an obvious 'hard nut' or just decide to let you go.

HITTING THE ROAD

Modern zombie survival thinking favours a range of vehicles for use during a zombie outbreak but at least one of these should be capable of the longer distances involved in a serious Bugging-Out operation.

Even if you aim to stay put, safely tucked up in your fortified home, things could change, prompting a need for you and your family to move on quickly. Imagine, for example, a wall collapsing and zombies or troublesome bandits intent on looting flooding into your garden. Perhaps there is a polluted water supply making your location untenable. You get the idea. Under these circumstances, we're talking about getting you, your party and supplies possibly hundreds of miles from your home base. This is going to take some serious planning. Most zombie preppers are very secretive about their own Bug-Out plans and you'll find little in the way of route maps or location detail on internet forums.

On our densely populated island, the 'obvious' locations are going to get busy quickly so it's worth crossing off sites such as the New Forest, other National Parks and 'heading for the Highlands'. These sites will be crowded with fellow survivors, bandits and, of course, the walking dead. You will need to be more creative, and vehicle selection will be key in guiding any Bug-Out Location decision. Something worth repeating is that you should always have more than one potential location. When considering longer-range Bug-Out Vehicles, focus naturally turns to vans, buses and coaches – larger vehicles with space to store the Bug-Out Supplies necessary for such a journey.

OPTION 1
CARAVANS

If the idea of facing the apocalypse towing a naff white caravan fills you with dread, your survival instincts are correct…
In general, caravans will reduce your carefully prepared Bug-Out Super-Vehicle to the status of an extra-cautious Sunday driver who is being even more cautious than normal as if they are attending some kind of antiques fair. The benefits of bringing your home with you are off-set by the impact on speed and performance. Don't do it, just don't. Go for a campervan/RV instead which offers better stability and road worthiness. A decent caravan could be an option if you have one in place as a hideout in the woods.

The end of the world is no place to try out your sparkling new Coachman Pastiche deluxe caravan regardless of how well its beds fold out or how many toilets it has.

OPTION 2
VANS

With strong frames and decent engines, there are a variety of vans which could be real assets during a zombie apocalypse. Choosing wisely will be the key. It's a very broad market with a few poorly designed and unreliable options out there but get it right and a decent quality van will be an excellent workhouse for carrying supplies. It will blend in well in urban landscapes and can easily be pimped out to become a quality zombie-bashing machine. There are plenty of case studies on the Internet of preppers converting vans into a 'recreational vehicle' or RV configuration, with beds and in-built storage. This often proves cheaper than buying a new RV.

Often over-looked by those new to zombie survival planning, a robust light commercial vehicle provides an excellent base from which to build a suitable Bug-Out Vehicle.

OPTION 3
HGVs

There are hundreds of forum threads discussing the various merits of converting a heavy goods vehicle into a zombie-busting tank and it is a valid point that with the right front protection, these powerful kings of the road could certainly do the business on the walking dead. However, there is less detail on them as long-range bug vehicles. Range is not typically an issue but navigating through our cluttered and blocked roads could present a bigger challenge. HGVs in all their configurations are still a valid option but need to be carefully considered in view of your own location and whether you or your team have the skills to drive one.

HGVs offer some real advantages but these benefits mean that inexperienced preppers tend to overlook the obvious drawbacks in terms of manoeuvrability.

HITTING THE ROAD
HAVE A PLAN

A Bug-Out Location can be something as simple as a secure hideout you can use during an emergency. Some will be very close to your home base. You may even plan to return to your home base once it's safe to do so.

Think of a long-term Bug-Out Location as a resettlement site – somewhere where you can start again, hopefully on more favourable terms with the conditions of the apocalypse. Talk about long-term Bug-Out Locations to any serious zombie survival planner and they're sure to go quiet. It's a personal thing and most prefer to keep their locations secret for obvious reasons. It's a professional courtesy as a fellow prepper to respect their privacy so don't probe.

Once you've decided on a location, remember to do dry runs and even start keeping small stocks of supplies for when things starting turning zombie.

OPTION 4
MILITARY VEHICLES

Forget tanks and many other armoured vehicles as most require specialist training, are very rare and have a surprisingly limited range. Hardy models – Army Land Rovers and armoured personnel carriers – are often stripped of unnecessary electrical clutter and have easy to maintain engines but they will be highly sought after. Some more well-organised groups will look to use vehicles such as the FV510 Warrior which, with its range of over 400 miles and useful 30 mm L21A1 cannon would prove a powerful protection vehicle for any convoy. In the early days, few groups will have the capacity or organisation to take out a vehicle such as a Warrior.

 If you are lucky enough to snag a military vehicle that has firepower then it's a good choice to protect any convoy. Support vehicles are the best targets – Land Rovers or supply lorries.

OPTION 5
RVs

The zombie survival community takes RVs very seriously and there are now a wide range of apocalypse vehicles available on the market. Even if you decide to purchase a 'civilian' model and convert, selecting an RV as your Bug-Out Vehicle is not a budget option and if you settle on a cheaper model, you'll suffer some of the same disadvantages as with a caravan – poor stability, wafer thin fibre-glass walls and a lack of defensive features. However, get things right and you'll have made a major step towards surviving the end times. This volume includes a detailed case study of an apocalypse RV – study the features and ensure your vehicle meets this standard.

 A solid, well-built RV is a complete survival vehicle and is a great Bug-Out Vehicle choice. Get the best model you can afford and go for a purpose-built survival vehicle if you can afford it.

OPTION 6
BUS/COACH

Buses and coaches come kitted out for 'life on board' with features such as washrooms, seats and even beds – such vehicles feature prominently on most 'Best Bug-Out Vehicle' lists. With a reliable bus or coach, you have the prospect of transporting your entire party plus supplies in one main vehicle, perhaps with a few outriders as escorts. That means 1 engine to maintain and 1 fuel gauge to watch, plus the strength of having your forces concentrated in one location. You do need to ensure that your vehicle has some basic defensive features such as a firing platform on top, wheel guards and some frontal protection for ramming.

 'Fortified' coaches remain a viable option as a larger Bug-Out Vehicle and there is plenty of content out there on survival forums about the conversion process. A good choice.

HITTING THE ROAD

PREPARING TO MOVE —

Any travel through 'bandit country' is dangerous but imagine leading a band of survivors including screaming toddlers and Auntie Vi with the dodgy leg. In addition, you will all be weighed down with any supplies you require for the journey. As with any convoy, you will move at the pace of your slowest member and although the walking dead are not long-distance runners they are capable of overrunning your limited party by sheer numbers. Any members of the party who fall behind will be at the mercy of the following pack of shuffling ghouls. Zombie survival experts cite poor preparation when Bugging-Out as the top cause of avoidable deaths during an apocalypse. No one will be keeping score at the end of the world but this lesson really is one to remember.

HITTING THE ROAD
TOP BUGGING-OUT TIPS

1 As with most areas of survival, planning is key but even preparing a basic movement plan can make for some daunting reading. For example, it will need to include any scouting plans, potential obstacles, your main routes and several alternative routes as they will doubtless be required.

2 You will need to assess your destination and agree any movement plan as well as planning for the unexpected. Tough choices will need to be made on which supplies to take and what to leave behind. The danger, risk and difficulty of travelling through zombie-infested country increases exponentially with the distance you travel. It is a grim calculation but if you push your party too far or beyond its capabilities, someone will end up getting eaten.

3 In 'undead' Britain, with roads mostly blocked and even key bridges and tunnels down, your party will probably only average 10–15 miles a day depending on factors such as fitness and ghoul activity. These figures will make long-trek hikes to remote locations such as National Parks or mountain areas an unrealistic objective for most parties.

4 It is good practice to identify at least 3 possible long-term locations before the zombies rise. You can then research these locations in the peace before the crisis and make the best assessment as to their long-term viability.

5 Do as much research as possible. Plot alternative routes and note any sites of potential interest en route. Specific locations will be reviewed in later sections but a good mix of types is important. Above all, do not leave with a general objective to say 'reach Scotland' or 'get to an island'.

6 Your groups should always have a reachable destination and route mapped out. Travel plans will need to change as you encounter the ghouls but your end goal should be clear or people will start to lose faith. Aimless wandering is also a quick way to get members of your party killed. If your current location is overrun and you need to leave in a hurry, head for your nearest Bug-Out Location and re-group before attempting the long-term move.

7 Your choice of long-term locations needs to reflect your party's ability to move so if you know you will be travelling with children or people with movement problems, you need to factor this in. Do not count on any motor vehicles, if you have them then brilliant but projections are that most carriageways will be blocked. Going by foot or bicycle are good options.

There are many possible scenarios but good planning around emergency bags, escape routes and Bug-Out locations, will give you a fighting chance to reach your long-term destination, even if you need to leave earlier than expected.

Emigration
Leaving the country?

Thinking of grabbing a boat and getting abroad? Experts predict that if one major country falls to the zombies, the others will follow closely on in a ghoulish domino effect. If you really desire a move, think through the logistics of even a relatively simple route across the English Channel or the Irish Sea. Also, will the desperate survivors in these locations be glad to see you?

Other Towns and Cities
Finding abandoned urban locations

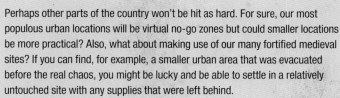

Perhaps other parts of the country won't be hit as hard. For sure, our most populous urban locations will be virtual no-go zones but could smaller locations be more practical? Also, what about making use of our many fortified medieval sites? If you can find, for example, a smaller urban area that was evacuated before the real chaos, you might be lucky and be able to settle in a relatively untouched site with any supplies that were left behind.

Retail Parks and Outlets
Classic zombie survival locations

Most towns and cities now have retail parks on the outskirts so you'd be looking at a much shorter Bug-Out journey. Ample supplies, good defensive potential and a choice of high street names – what's not to love? Well, if you think that way so will other groups of survivors and bandits. Expect organised gangs to hit these locations and become very protective over other survivors moving in on their 'turf'.

Military Base
Safe and secure?

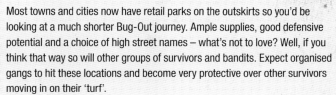

Reinforced steel outer perimeters and the mouth-watering prospect of military vehicles and weapons make these sites an attractive choice. But, remember, these locations are most likely to be a venue for many 'last stands' as the brave remnants of the army and desperate survivors battle to the end. Expect these locations to be infested with zombies and the supplies long-since exhausted. Worth a scout but don't expect to settle.

Going Underground
Living like a Morlock

You may be lucky enough to have or know about a secure and prepared luxury bunker. The rumour is that the government has them all over the place. More likely, you'll be facing life in a dark and damp basement-type affair. Bunkers and caves are typically hard to find, plus you'll still need to keep your transportation handy for regular foraging trips. If the kids start developing large saucer eyes, it's time to move on.

'The Country'
Green wellies and the occasional zombie

Most often cited as a Bug-Out location but in reality you are rarely far from an urban centre in most of the UK. There are areas such as our National Parks but factor in that you'll be sharing the Lake District with thousands of refugees from the North West. Similarly, the Highlands will be overrun with survivors from Glasgow and Edinburgh – you get the idea…

Islands
Protected by the sea or marooned?

Luckily, the UK and Ireland is surrounded by thousands of islands and islets, which could provide a refuge from the zombie chaos. The bad news is that many are remote and tend to be in the north. An alternative may be one of the many artificial platforms dotted around our coast, such as oil rig platforms.

NOTE: LONG-TERM SETTLEMENT LOCATIONS ARE COVERED IN MORE DETAIL IN THE HAYNES *ZOMBIE SURVIVAL MANUAL*, 2013

HITTING THE ROAD

LONG-DISTANCE TRAVEL

Regardless of how discreetly you move, the journey of any party of live humans will attract the attention of hungry ghouls and before too long ongoing defences will be required. It is important to remember, however, that you are not on a crusade against the dead. Your operating guideline is to travel as quietly as possible avoiding hordes where you can and minimising any encounters. You may need to lengthen your journey to go around urban areas or zombie crowds, for example.

You may also encounter bands of remaining humans who will have become increasingly desperate as their struggle to survive gets harder and harder. Again, avoid encounters if you can by staying clear of the most obvious foraging locations such as shopping complexes or town centres.

If you should directly encounter any other bands of humans, exercise extreme caution. Be friendly where possible and help those in need but be firm. Desperate times will create desperate people. Be sceptical of outsiders; your party will depend on your judgement. If there is any element of confrontation back down if you can and retreat with your supplies and party intact. You should be prepared to fight if rivals attack.

▶ HOW TO STAY ALIVE IN THE WASTELAND

The following guidelines should become second nature as your party transits through 'bandit country' and are the basics of taking a group through zombie-infested areas. Know your group well before you leave and allocate roles to match people's skills. Ensure everyone has a job and knows what is expected of them. There won't be any time for debate once you're out in zombieland.

'ONCE CIVILISATION HAS COLLAPSED, LONG-DISTANCE TRAVEL WON'T BE FOR THE POORLY PREPARED. PREPARE CAREFULLY. PLAN IN DETAIL. BE READY TO FIGHT AT ALL TIMES'
DAWN JAMES, MOODY'S SURVIVOR GROUP

STEP 1
ALWAYS CHECK VEHICLES

Ensure that you regularly check your main vehicles and be prepared to evacuate one if it goes 'out of action' for any reason. This means ensuring that vital supplies are spread across vehicles and that you have the capacity to lose any one vehicle. Vehicle breakdowns are the most likely source of trouble so ensure that you have a generally understood operating guideline – such as 'if it can be repaired in a few hours, we'll do it, if not; we abandon it and move on'.

STEP 2
AN EFFECTIVE DEFENCE

All of your party should have some form of defence, like an effective melee weapon, for example, and have the skills to use it. There may be exceptions to this such as very small children or the sick but you must maximise your anti-ghoul arsenal and discourage roving bands of humans from taking advantage. Remember to distribute your best warriors in the convoy system outlined.

HITTING THE ROAD

SCOUTING METHODS

A good technique when heading out on any long-term travel is to use a forward scout to try out potential routes and highlight risks and obstacles before the main party arrives.

▶ Travelling up to a day in front, this pathfinder will check routes and propose changes to avoid blockages. A useful technique is where the guide leaves prominent marks in spray paint along the route to guide the following party. Off-road motorbikes are ideal where longer distances are involved but the noise can be an issue. Bicycles are quieter but slower and have a shorter-range.

▶ Your scout should be fit and a strong fighter. They should be lightly provisioned and armed but their main objective is stealth and research, not engagement. This role demands as much patience as it does strength so discount any gung-ho Rambo types.

▶ With a realistic target location, a good scout may be able to review an entire route to your new location and even transport small quantities of supplies. Other activities may include doing a quick sweep of your target location or preparing a strong point to provide a safe base in your new area. If your party is large enough, then using a scout is strongly recommended.

STEP 3
SPEED IS AN ADVANTAGE

Do not be tempted to over-load your vehicles or party with supplies. In most scenarios, speed will be your principle advantage over the shuffling undead so do not negate this advantage. If necessary, transport supplies on separate runs or, if this is not possible, simply be ruthless with the amount. Over-burdening key members of your team who need to serve on defensive duties could be fatal to your party.

STEP 4
CONTACT STRATEGY

You and your party must develop and agree a 'contact strategy' for when you encounter the walking dead. For example, the military make good use of pre-agreed hand signals to communicate information from the soldier on point. It is vital that the whole party understands when to stay silent and even when to scatter. A simple set of agreed guidelines in areas such as dealing with an unexpected encounter will greatly increase your chances of survival.

BE AWARE THAT APPEARANCES CAN BE DECEPTIVE

It is possible that you and your party will enter an apparently empty area only to be confronted by ghouls swarming from every building. Do not assume this is some kind of ambush or that the zombies have developed some way to co-ordinate an attack, it is far more likely that no matter how quiet your party is, their noise or the scent of live humans has just taken time to reach the dormant ghouls. A good way to avoid this is to use a forward scout to make a significant noise and check out a route, as long as he or she can safely exit if numerous ghouls emerge.

HITTING THE ROAD

ZOMBIE APOCALYPSE RV

Campervans or RVs are superb Bug-Out Vehicles but getting a good rig is not cheap and even the best non-purpose RVs need some adaptions to ensure they are zombie-safe. For example, most regular RVs have extremely thin fibreglass or plastic walls – these certainly need strengthening. As a general guideline, it's better to buy than rent and be prepared for some high petrol bills as you practice your zombie outbreak evacuation plans. Go for the best machine you can afford – if necessary spend more on a robust frame then add homemade zombie defences.

A great strength of RVs and similar vehicles is that you can pretty much carry everything with you. Also, if you have the right supplies, you hardly need to stop, therefore greatly reducing your chances of running into the walking dead. One thing to remember though is to watch the weight of your vehicle, particularly when you start factoring in supplies attached to the roof, any armour or shielding and additional fuel tanks.

You can also look at converting light commercial or heavy goods vehicles into RV-type configurations by building in living spaces and defences.

▶ MULTICAT ZOMBIECROSS 60 'THE WINCHESTER'

The perfect Mad Max-style post-apocalyptic cruiser is ideal if you're travelling solo, or plan to rule the zombie wasteland as a mysterious street warrior, but what if you're stuck in a 3-bedroom semi, have 2.4 kids and a 9–5 office job? How can you get your travel needs sorted short of soldering armour plates to the aging people carrier you use for the school run? Well, the answer is the Multicat Zombiecross 60 series – an all-terrain purpose-built family survival vehicle. Before you imagine a camouflage expedition vehicle which is going to stick out in suburbia, this series is designed to look just like a regular recreational vehicle or RV. Read on but be prepared to dig out those forms about taking a second mortgage because this kind of zombie stopping power doesn't come cheap!

'OUR DAUGHTER AMELLIA HAS BECOME QUITE THE EXPERT WITH ALL THE ON-BOARD ZOMBIE DEFENCES SUCH AS MANAGING THE MOVEMENT DETECTION SENSOR ARRAYS'
MR MASON, END OF DAYS CARAVANS

THE MASON FAMILY ZOMBIE SURVIVAL PLAN
End of Days (EoD) Caravans, Tampa, Florida

LOCATION
Mr Mason (location withheld). EoD has a showroom in Tampa Bay, Florida, with over 25 models on display.

PURPOSE
'This is our family's apocalypse survival plan. We went for the zombie variation as we thought this was the most likely cause of the end of the world. But, whatever it is – zombies, aliens, the collapse of the economy – this vehicle is going to get us to our Bug-Out Location deep in the New Forest. We've owned it for about 3 years now and have used it every year for holidays both here and abroad.'

TECHNICAL SPECIFICATIONS
6 litre, 6-cylinder diesel engine, 320 horsepower and 9-speed manual transmission. All-wheel drive with central lock differential. Sealed anti-ghoul drum brakes. 365/80 R 45 Michelin Zomb-XL tubeless tyres. Dimensions – length 7.5 metres, width 2.35 metres, height 2.90 metres. Fully-laden weight 4,000 kg.

ARMAMENTS
None as standard but military packs can be ordered where it is legal to do so in your country. This version is fitted with a range of anti-zombie features. EoD Caravans reports that one owner in Texas has fitted twin M60s to their machine plus a quick-fire anti-tank weapon.

RANGE
With double 600 litre fuel tanks, 600–800 miles depending on road conditions. Maximum speed of around 75 mph.

CREW
4–8 persons – can accommodate 12 plus supplies but not in any comfort and this would include several survivors riding shotgun on the roof. Most models can also be fitted with a specially designed Bug-Out Supplies trailer.

BUDGET
£85,000 for the standard version of the Multicat Zombiecross 60 – 'The Winchester'. Weapons packs come in at around £10,000 each including 4 AK-47z with ammunition boxes, EoD Caravans don't make budget models so all of the components meet military-grade specifications.

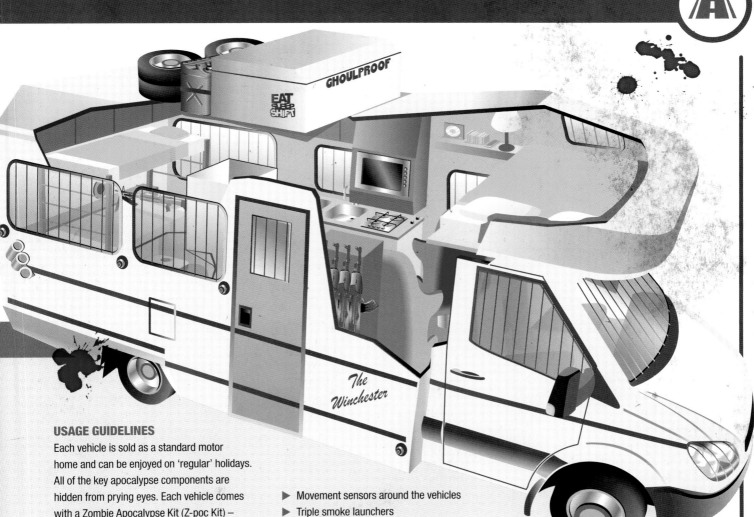

USAGE GUIDELINES

Each vehicle is sold as a standard motor home and can be enjoyed on 'regular' holidays. All of the key apocalypse components are hidden from prying eyes. Each vehicle comes with a Zombie Apocalypse Kit (Z-poc Kit) – consisting of the steel bull bars to protect the front of the vehicle plus around a dozen other anti-zombie and raider fortifications. This is so that 'The Winchester' can be easily converted once things start getting toasty.

FEATURES

- ▶ Robust 9-speed manual 'all-terrain' transmission with military-grade sealed gearbox and 'long-life' oil filtering system
- ▶ Purpose designed anti-ghoul braking system, calibrated to clear up to 4 litres of zombie gunk per mile
- ▶ Hardened R 45 Michelin Zomb-XL tyres – tough enough to handle any road conditions. Wheels also include a patented coded quick release mechanism
- ▶ 26 storage compartments across the vehicle including 10 lockable and 3 hidden storage spaces

- ▶ Movement sensors around the vehicles
- ▶ Triple smoke launchers
- ▶ Fully tinted, toughened glass windows
- ▶ Self-supporting UNICAT sandwich plate panels of fortified zombie-proof fibreglass composite
- ▶ Under body emergency escape hatch
- ▶ Top hatch and light machine gun firing port
- ▶ Extended emergency fuel tank
- ▶ Seating area for 4–6 persons, with adjustable swivelling table on pedestal in the front of the cabin
- ▶ Seating unit converts to additional double bed
- ▶ Combined sealed shower and toilet room with door to isolate from living area
- ▶ Oven with microwave and deep apocalypse-class 150 litre fridge
- ▶ Overhead cupboards above kitchen units and emergency food rations
- ▶ LPG 4-flame stove
- ▶ 800 litre freeze-proof drinking water tanks

- ▶ Waste water tank – capacity 175 litres
- ▶ Diesel powered warm water central heating (7 kW)
- ▶ High radiant heat share due to radiators in living area, sanitary room and bed area
- ▶ Bicycle carrier at rear
- ▶ Spare wheel carrier at the rear and on the roof
- ▶ Off the grid 1000E washing machine
- ▶ Water filtration system
- ▶ Roof slots and floor restraints to enable an additional storage unit or firing platform to be fitted to the roof and which can be accessed by either a ladder at the rear or an optional internal roof hatch.

HITTING THE ROAD

ZOMBIE BATTLE BUS

There is significant interest in the zombie prepping community around converting vehicles into 'battle buses' – that is long-range, armoured and armed moving bases, which can cope with both zombies and the dangerous conditions in the wasteland. Here we profile a London Routemaster bus conversion.

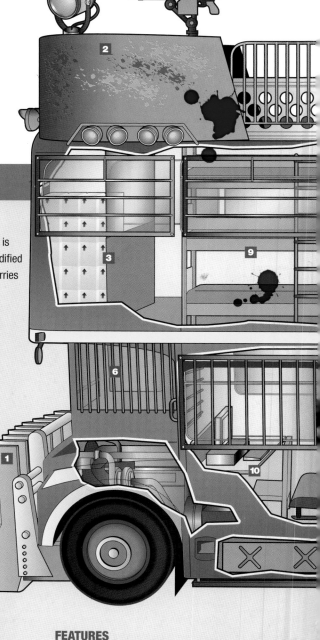

▶ THE ROUTEMASTER APOCALYPSE BUS

Iconic and instantly recognisable, many will be surprised to learn that the original designers of the famous Routemaster bus in the late 1940s had always planned a post-apocalyptic version. Unfortunately, only fragmentary plans exist for their Cold War 'Battle Bus' but models assembled before 1978 were indeed built on a military-grade chassis, providing a vehicle strength far beyond what is normal.

THE ROUTEMASTER APOCALYPSE BUS

Mrs Wakely, Boggy Bottom, Hertfordshire

LOCATION

Hidden in a local barn, safe from prying village nose-poker-inners.

PURPOSE

Long-range post-apocalyptic transporter and live-in bastion

TECHNICAL SPECIFICATIONS

1965 RM2120 Routemaster (restored), original front suspension, power steering and automatic gearbox. 1972 Leyland 10 litre Supra-Diesel Engine. All aluminium stressed skin construction. Complete interior rebuild.

ARMAMENTS

2 hand guns from World War 1, 1 fowling piece, Grandad's shotgun and a set of vintage golf clubs.

RANGE

The standard capacity on a Routemaster is around 130 Litres – this model has a modified tank with a capacity of 200 litres plus carries a full set of 5-gallon safety jerry cans. With modifications made to the engine, it can do 7 miles to the gallon so without using emergency supplies and at a steady speed of 30 mph, it can do just over 300 miles.

CREW

'We've built it for the family plus a few neighbours. That's a crew of 12–14.'

BUDGET

'Our model was in particularly good condition and we paid £71,000 for her. There are cheaper vehicles out there. If you plan to convert it, ensure that it's a pre-1977 model.'

USAGE GUIDELINES

'We plan to use our bus as a Bug-Out Vehicle. We've found a secluded beach in Devon which will be easy to seal off from the zombies. We plan to head there then use the bus as our home. We increased our fuel tank size and spent a tidy sum on it. Luckily, I had a bingo win so spent the cash on getting a specialist in to complete the work. Always go for the older models as they are easier to maintain.'

FEATURES

1 A reinforced steel front scoop, built to clear any obstruction, be it broken down cars or zombie hordes. The scoop is detachable and can be stored on the roof, which improves the vehicles off-road performance.

2 Front and rear integrated armoured weapons stations, both shown with a modified FN Herstal light machine gun, with 100 round disintegrating belts.

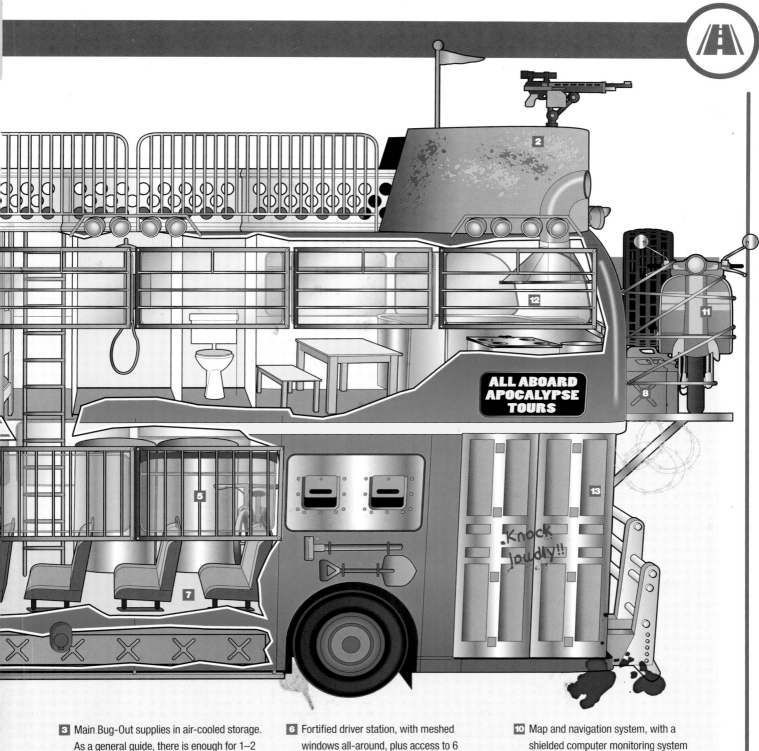

3 Main Bug-Out supplies in air-cooled storage. As a general guide, there is enough for 1–2 months of supplies for a party of 10–14 survivors. Fresh food is stored in under-floor tanks in different sections of the vehicle.

4 A directional spotter lamp with integrated infra-red and 'Zombie Cool-Vision' camera.

5 Two vast 100 litre armoured fuel tanks, enabling a fully-laden vehicle to complete around 300 miles without refuelling.

6 Fortified driver station, with meshed windows all-around, plus access to 6 internal and external CCTV cameras.

7 Travel seating for 8 survivors, with under-seat storage.

8 Emergency external fuel reserves and spare wheel tool station, everything required to keep the bus on the road.

9 6-berth sleeping cabin – typically used as 'hotbeds' for survivors.

10 Map and navigation system, with a shielded computer monitoring system of on-board systems.

11 50cc Honda moped, used for foraging.

12 Kitchen and canteen area with full specification refrigerator unit, quad-hob, oven and storage.

13 Fortified steel concertina folding doors, with viewing port. Alternative exits include a floor hatch to escape under the vehicle.

HITTING THE ROAD

SURVIVOR GROUPS

As time progresses, the mix of who is on the road after a major zombie outbreak is going to change. The first few weeks will be dominated by unprepared survivors, desperate emergency services and the occasional remnants of a military unit. This period won't last long and soon you will find yourself sharing the post-apocalyptic roadway with a diverse array of potentially dangerous groups. It is vital that you consider the main survivor profiles and be able to recognise their vehicles and their battle tactics. The Ministry of Zombies developed a set of survivor profiles, which has since been adopted by many in the zombie survival community as an 'industry-standard'. As with any profiling, these are generalised and survivors will no doubt encounter mixed and hybrid groups. Nevertheless, these profiles are helpful, particularly in terms of your offensive and defensive driving tactics against such opponents.

'WE WILL ONLY START TO SEE THE EMERGENCE OF THE MORE ORGANISED EXTREME GROUPS AROUND THREE MONTHS AFTER Z-DAY, WHEN THE LAST VESTIGES OF LAW AND ORDER AND SOCIETAL BARRIERS HAVE BEEN WELL AND TRULY BROKEN'
DR RAYMOND CARTER, PROFESSOR OF VIROLOGY

WITHIN ONE MONTH OF Z-DAY

Unprepared survivors, panicking individuals and any remaining military or police units. They will be scattering from the main urban centres, road chaos, ad-hoc looting and outbreaks of violence on the roads.

ONE–THREE MONTHS AFTER Z-DAY

Opportunistic criminal gangs will become more organised, the remaining survivors will be more 'zombie-hardened' and fragmented military or police units will disintegrate or transform. The great escape from urban centres is over. Looting is more organised. Vehicles will start to appear more adapted to the end of the world. Expect a large number of motorcycles as easily available fuel starts to become scarcer.

MORE THAN THREE MONTHS AFTER

Dominant criminal gangs will start to organise into structured robber baron groups. Hardcore wasteland warriors will remain but in too few numbers to defend survivors against any number of bizarre groupings such as cannibals and possibly mutants. This is when the true wasteland will emerge. Expect violent organised groups, battles over fuel and Mad Max-style innovations on the road. In many ways, the roads will be more dangerous than in the first weeks of the apocalypse.

 ## HITTING THE ROAD
ENCOUNTERING SURVIVORS

Be particularly aware of any lone humans you come across as they may have been thrown out or escaped from their own party after becoming infected.

These dangerous individuals will be keen to try to integrate into your party and an enemy within is the most dangerous as they will already be within your security perimeter. They will disguise the fact that they are infected by either trying to blot it out or by hoping in vain for some kind of recovery. If they turn up at night, then they will cause serious problems for your party. Treat any newcomer with caution but also remember that they may genuinely be alone and could bring valuable new skills into your party. Just keep a close eye on them at first.

► SURVIVOR GROUP PROFILES

	MOST LIKELY TO BE FOUND	THEIR TACTICS	YOUR TACTICS
The Great Unprepared 'We don't need no help'	Aimlessly foraging, trying to find a way to survive. Most likely on foot or stolen BMX.	Typically passive. If they attack, it will be panicky, uncoordinated and desperate, particularly if they see your Bug-Out Gear and decide you look vulnerable enough.	Leave them in peace if you can. These lost souls are those unprepared for the end of the world and they've got enough on their plate. If they are foolish enough to attack, sit back and bat them away like flies.
Generation Zee 'OMG! I am so gonna skin you alive!'	Hanging around post-apocalyptic corners, waiting for burnt out branches of McDonalds to re-open.	Swarm attacks, particularly on lone targets. Generation Z will always look for signs of weakness and will attack if they feel 'dissed'. As the months progress, this group will become more unpredictable and violent.	Avoid eye contact, ensure that you are as big a target as possible and therefore costly to attack. Back away if necessary, ensuring that you cover your retreat. Do not confront or challenge unless you have over-whelming force. If in combat, target the ring-leaders.
Wasteland Warriors 'I used to work in a call centre'	Patrolling the wastelands and towns, often looking for some kind of 'mission'.	These warriors will gravitate towards trouble then engage fiercely to defend helpless survivors. They will often pull surprise weapons from their vehicles and fight to the end.	Don't attack any helpless survivors whilst these drivers are around. Play it cool. A subtle nod of the head with perhaps an admiring glance will normally see you through. This group often has a plucky sidekick or sturdy dog.
Travelling Survivors 'I'm outta water, let's be friends?'	Our crumbling motorways and A roads, heading for that elusive 'safe zone'.	Will corral if attacked into an old-fashioned defensive circle. Expect the occasional firearm.	Convoys of traveller are unlikely to attack unless they're really desperate. As the months progress, those left will be battle-hardened and up for a fight if required. Avoid unless you want to be exposed to their extensive 'back story'. You'll soon learn that everyone alive after the apocalypse has a 'story'.
Robber Barons 'I'll take those supplies'	Foraging warehouses, threatening survivor communities and generally trying to expand their 'empires'.	Full on, likely to have firearms, be battle-hardened and able to call on reinforcements. Likely to include some ex-military, tactics will be sophisticated and organised, such as flanking.	Avoid if at all possible. Stay away from their known territories, looting locations and bases. Don't steal their parking spaces. If you are captured, you are most likely to be asked to 'pledge' your allegiance. Robber Barons themselves typically carry some kind of token weapon like a cricket-bat covered in barbed wire.
Apocalypse Amazons 'Multi-tasking to the end of the world'	The better shopping malls and city centres. Any boutique that hasn't been burnt out. Any tea-shops still open.	VW beetles, with post-apocalypse pimpage. Numerous small cars, with the occasional Chelsea tractor (premium SUV). This group doesn't typically attack but if do, expect an organised and swift 'swarm' style assault.	You leave them alone, they'll leave you alone. Whatever you do don't tailgate an amazon convoy. If find them in a deserted high street, just let them finish. You can de-escalate any confrontation by directing them to an unlooted brand-name shop they may not be aware of.
Cannibals 'You look so sweaty and tasty'	Either their settlements or known combat black spots. Cannibals also favour hospitals and other medical locations.	Will avoid conflict against stronger opponents. In combat, will leave vehicle attack with blunt and bladed weapons. Often fights as a family group so expect to be attacked by everyone from Granny to baby Caleb.	Be strong, try to look as powerful as possible and wear slimming clothes. Try not to look too tasty – for example, sweating profusely can give you that 'just basted' look which cannibals find appetising. Equally, having long, greasy hair can ensure you look less 'appealing'.
Ex-military/ Robocops 'Respect my authority maggot!'	Key foraging locations such as warehouses, military bases and along their convoy routes.	Similar to Robber Baron groups but these guys are well-trained in close protection and vehicular combat. They are skilful drivers, typically working as part of a team.	Avoid if possible. Less trigger happy and ambitious than organised bandits but they may still 'liberate' your vehicle if they fancy it. Do not appear to be a threat if you meet one of their convoys but keep one hand on your gun in case things get toasty.
End of the World Scientists 'Quick, I've run out of test tubes!'	Mad loners, locked in their homes. If outside, they'll be found in some specialist supply or shops.	Mad loners avoid others by choice, unless they start some lunatic quest to 'cleanse the earth' – which will probably happen at some point. If they do, expect something akin to the child-catcher from *Chitty Chitty Bang Bang*.	Will only attack if they absolutely have to or are driven to either by a need for supplies or the voices in their head. Their targets will be those alone or vulnerable. Be firm and make it known you are armed and both groups will think twice. If they are foraging for supplies, just leave them to it.

NOTE: SURIVOR GROUPS ARE COVERED IN MORE DETAIL IN THE HAYNES *ZOMBIE SURVIVAL MANUAL*, 2013

TRAVELLING BY WATER

Most parts of the UK are within reach of the coast, river or one of our recently much-improved canals or waterways. Plus, anything more than a puddle can be a real challenge for the average zombie.

Easy access to a river or waterway could greatly increase your ability to forage and explore further afield. For example, you could use river transport to reach some key supply locations such as large retail stores or warehouses rather than risking a more dangerous road route.

There are countless books and courses which can teach you river craft or how to handle your new small boat but few will prepare you for the unique challenges of the zombies. You must be prepared for the numerous floating corpses which are expected in the aftermath of the ghoul rising and the grim possibility of blocked rivers. Forget any ideas of a pleasant river cruise, there will be the constant threat of ghouls clawing at your paddle or dropping from low bridges. You will need to be vigilant and silent as you move through the water.

WATER ACCESS REQUIRED

Few homes in the UK have direct and secure access to a waterway so chances are you will need to lift and carry your boat to the water's edge. This doesn't sound too traumatic but in reality this could be a very dangerous exercise. If you are lucky enough to live somewhere that backs onto a river then don't forget that you will still need to 'secure' your access with strong anti-ghoul fencing.

IS TRAVELLING ON WATER SAFE?

It really depends. A waterway clogged with dismembered crawlers, floating limbless wonders and the occasional bloater on the bank is a far from safe place but water is certainly no friend to the clumsy dead. With sensible precautions, most water forms of transport will be preferable to facing the hungry hordes on dry land. As a general rule, the deeper the water, the safer you'll be.

OPTION 1
SMALL DINGY

In terms of reliable and practical river transport, you will struggle to beat a wooden or fibreglass 2–3 man dingy, which can be bought for around £200 and will provide you with an easy to control craft in which 2 team members could head out in to forage and still have room to bring back valuable suppliers.

Robust and hardy, these crafts are typically light weight and could be easily carried to the water's edge when required. If you decide to use a motorised version, you will need to carefully consider the noise implications against the advantages in terms of distance travelled. Choose a boat with high sides if possible to resist grabbing water zombies.

You need to be physically fit to operate any boat using oars over longer distances so ensure that you get out on the river for training. Some survivalists prefer short kayak paddles to oars as they are more difficult for zombies to grab hold off as you move through the water.

OPTION 2
INLAND MOTOR CRUISER

As an example, there are hundreds of pleasure craft available on locations such as the Norfolk Broads where there are hundreds of miles of navigable waterways and some excellent remote rural locations to moor. The older boats often hired out for holidays are like flat-bottomed floating caravans and are designed to take up to 12 people in relative comfort. With dependable diesel engines and a robust fibreglass build, these crafts could easily provide a floating bastion for you and your team.

Better still, if you can purchase and secure a boat before the zombies arrive, you can stockpile fuel and supplies ready for the crisis. You will then be able to head out to a secure bug out location, moor up and see the crisis through in comfort whilst doing a spot of fishing.

It should be noted that most of the boats on the UK's inland waterways are not designed for the open water of the sea but can if stocked up to provide an excellent alternative to a fixed land location.

TRAVELLING BY WATER
GET THE RIGHT TRAINING

Before getting carried away, it is important to understand that all types of crafts, bar the very smallest dingy, will need some degree of specialist training, if not to steer then at least to maintain. Consider the treacherous currents around our coast and the problems you may experience navigating, and you will realise that boats are not something you can just jump into.

Whichever craft you select, it is important that you get some experience on the river before the dead rise. Thousands of people enjoy canoeing around the country and it is an ideal way to learn the rivers and waterways in your location. It may be that these routes offer you a more secure trip to a long-term location, for example, in which case, you will need to seriously think about accommodating the whole party and supplies. The options below present some different solutions, including the possibility of securing a much larger vessel that could double as a floating base as well as a form of transport. Don't discount commercial boats as they are often over-looked in favour of more expensive and well-equipped private cruisers.

SEAFARING AND SAILING SKILLS NEED TO BE LEARNT, THEY CANNOT JUST BE PICKED UP IN A FEW HOURS

OPTION 3
YACHT

Yachts or any sea-going vessels require a substantially bigger investment in terms of money and resources than say fibreglass canoes or smaller craft. The market for private vessels is a very broad one with prices ranging from £4,000 for a used single diesel engine boat, which will still have a kind of floating caravan feel, to the multi-million pound super yachts of the rich and famous, which often include their own pools and be over 160 metres in length.

The good news is that there is a well-established used boat market in the UK with prices to suit most budgets. For example, the £4,000 mentioned above could easily secure you a reasonable 10-metre long vessel with a single cabin and which is capable of up to 6 knots. With 50-litre fresh water tanks and sails to use, it's possible to effectively manage fuel consumption and therefore such a vehicle would be quite capable of long-distance travel – you could easily head out to sea and spend a few relaxing months, waiting for the chaos to 'die' down.

OPTION 4
COMMERCIAL VESSELS

As you move up the vessel price range, new options open up to the zombie survivalist. Even if you mark the luxury yacht market as unrealistic, there is a whole range of medium-priced vessels, which although still require a serious financial investment, will provide you with one of the most secure mobile living spaces in zombie Britain. One example is a converted commercial whaler which is on the market for around £190,000 – a substantial commitment for most people.

This particular vessel is over 25 metres long and offers 6 cabins with additional living and storage space. It is a sea-going vessel and a rough calculation on fuel capacity indicates that it could do over 24,000 km on 1 full tank of fuel. It is possible, particularly if you are part of a larger survival team, that you could pool your resources as this vessel would easily accommodate 15 to 20 people. This opens up the possible strategy of heading to sea for the first few months of the zombie apocalypse and then carefully exploring the coast in the months that follow.

TRAVELLING BY WATER

ZOMBIES AND WATER

The dead avoid deep water where possible and they certainly can't swim. This does not necessarily make any lake or river a ghoul-free zone though as they can float in the water and are more than capable of clambering up onto most boats. However, it does mean that if you have access to either the sea or one of our major river or canal systems, then Bugging-Out by water should be investigated.

One aspect that survivors often don't consider is that immersion in water does change the appearance of the walking dead. Bodies typically display a greater degree of ruination and rotting. Green 'fungus' can cover the entire corpse and gases bloat zombies up into significantly larger creatures. Over a period

of time, the dead can take on a putrid 'sea-monster' appearance which can shock survivors.

It's almost impossible to prepare survivors for this marine form of ghoul shock. Just remember some basic combat moves and try to disregard their putrid appearance.

For example, an overhead bash is a powerful move almost certain to take out a zombie attacker providing you use a strong, reinforced paddle. The Stab 'n' Poke is an alternative and involves using a paddle or oar to simply jab or push the dead away from the boat.

With each manoeuvre the objective is to get the ghoul away from the boat and make your escape. Don't become another victim of marine ghoul shock.

▶ A GUIDE TO ZOMBIES IN WATER

TYPE 1
WADERS AND FLOUNDERERS

Experienced zombie fighters often say that shallow water is more dangerous as the dead mill around in water a few feet deep, ready to pounce on any passing human or boat. The water is deep enough to slow the living down and give the clumsy dead a fighting chance of a quick meat snack.

TYPE 2
THE FLOATING DEAD

Most zombie bodies float – meaning they'll drift as quickly as the current takes them, often becoming blocked at narrow points or shallows. Even if you make it to an island, you'll never be truly safe as one of the floating dead could wash ashore at any time. Many corpses can also clamber aboard any boat or raft which sits low enough in the water.

TRAVELLING BY WATER
ZOMBIES AND WATER

The Ministry of Zombies Transport Committee published an educational leaflet in early 2017 particularly targeted at educating survivors on the dangers and limitations of zombies and water. Here are some of the key questions:

CAN ZOMBIES SWIM?
We can confirm that zombies cannot swim. They lack the dexterity and the mental capacity to carry out even the most basic swimming stroke. They can wade through shallow water but once it reaches above their waist they are in danger of tipping and floating off. The frequent eye witness accounts of 'swimming zombies' are often floating torsos that have re-animated and now have flaying arms which can suggest the impression of a creature swimming.

ARE ZOMBIES SCARED OF WATER?
Zombies have no emotions as we understand them and are therefore not 'scared' of anything. What is being referred to here is a curious reaction that some of the walking dead have exhibited when confronted with a body of water as an obstacle, particularly if they can see a living human on the other side. Their overriding desire is to feast on the flesh of the living but their limited brain capacity is sometimes confused by the water in front of them.

DO ZOMBIES SINK?
It is true that saturated zombies in heavily waterlogged clothes will generally sink to the bottom. But, typically, currents prevent them from shambling along as normal. However, it should be noted that zombies do not require respiration to exist and therefore it is possible for these creatures to 'stay alive' whilst trapped underwater.

TYPE 3
BOTTOM FEEDERS
Some of the dead sink for a reason – they may be wearing heavy body armour or a massive rucksack, for example – and others just become drenched. We may not yet understand the science but the river or ocean bed is not a zombie-free zone and many swimmers will be caught unawares by these carnivorous bottom-feeders.

TYPE 4
BLOATERS
Bloaters are zombies which have, through an internal accumulation of acid and gas, become over-sized, often with vast protruding stomachs. More common in humid climates, these creatures can sometimes be found close to rivers and canals – particularly if the weather is warm. Bloaters are slower moving than a typical zombie.

TRAVELLING BY WATER

BUGGING-OUT BY CANOE

For a light and fast option, a well-designed, strong plastic touring or expedition canoe will cost between £400 and £600 and is a craft purposely designed for longer-distance travel. Modern canoes and kayaks can come with all sorts of accessories such as special fixed storage containers etc. What is common to all of these types of small boats is their shallow draft in the water, which will enable you to move on most waterways even if they are only a few feet deep. They can, however, be vulnerable to tipping so you should buy a newer outrigger anti-zombie model such as the Zomboe range. It is possible to modify a standard kayak by fitting an outrigger array but it's a complex job and will involve some specialist tools and skills.

CANOES AND KAYAKS

► Combat against human opponents is nigh on impossible from a canoe – particularly if they are armed. If your opponent is stronger or in greater numbers, attempt to escape by water. If you have to fight, make a landing, unseen if possible, then get stuck in. Be extra careful around bridges etc where either bandits or zombies could drop and even overturn your vessel.

► Canoes and other boats as Bug-Out Vehicles can be used for the journey but can't possibly be permanent locations. Sooner or later you will need a land base for supplies and repairs. Outrigger canoes are stable and perfect for these kinds of journeys but travelling beyond 100 miles, depending on conditions and levels of fitness, is unlikely.

► ZOMBOE 250 SERIES

The Zomboe 250 series is the world's first purpose-built zombie apocalypse outrigger canoe and is built by the Hawaii Watercraft Association in Honolulu. A high-performance, ultra-narrow underwater shaped canoe, a zombie-canoe or Zomboe comes in 1 and 2 person variants, both capable of taking survivors long distances across closed and open waters. Importantly, the outrigger adds the much needed stability that has blighted canoe and kayak forms of transport in zombie testing, where the ghoul simply unbalances the boat.

'AS A PROUD ISLAND PEOPLE WE ARE WELL PLACED TO SURVIVE A MAJOR ZOMBIE OUTBREAK. AND, THE ZOMBOE RANGE GIVES US THE KAYAKS AND CANOES TO DO IT IN'
DUKE AKAKA, PRESIDENT OF HAWAIAN WALKING DEAD DEFENSE GROUP

ZOMBOE 250 SERIES
Hawaii Watercraft Association, Honolulu

PURPOSE
If you plan to use canals, rivers or coastal waters to escape the zombies, this is the ideal cruiser. Stable in the water and fully equipped with emergency supplies, a Zomboe 250 will get you to your Bug-Out Location and can easily be converted into a light raider or patrol boat.

TECHNICAL SPECIFICATIONS
100% carbon layup, titanium shaft, high density foam ocre, one piece monocoque construction plus hybrid anti-zombie marine paint. Length 21", beam 16''. Hull weight 19lbs.

ARMAMENTS
Waterproof storage point for handgun. Metal reinforced paddle plus spare.

RANGE
Zombie apocalypse canoeing is very challenging, requiring excellent levels of fitness. In ideal conditions, an experienced rower can travel 2–4 miles per hour.

CREW
1–2 in basic models. Also available in 8-berth models.

BUDGET
Basic model for 1 person £3,000, with zombie apocalypse survival pack. 2-berth variants from £4,000. Larger bespoke vessels require pricing on project basis. All prices are plus delivery. (Firearm options available where legal depending on country of buyer.)

USAGE GUIDELINES
All survival canoes and kayaks are short-range boats in practical terms simply due to human limitations. They can be used for longer journeys but only with planning. These types of journeys will involve frequent camps and stops, as well as the constant vigilance of being in water with possible floating zombie threats. Fighting zombies from a boat is challenging at best and flight is often the best policy. You are also vulnerable to armed human raiders and combat against such opponents is better handled ashore. Skirting the coast can be a useful tactic as you can monitor for any potential foraging locations.

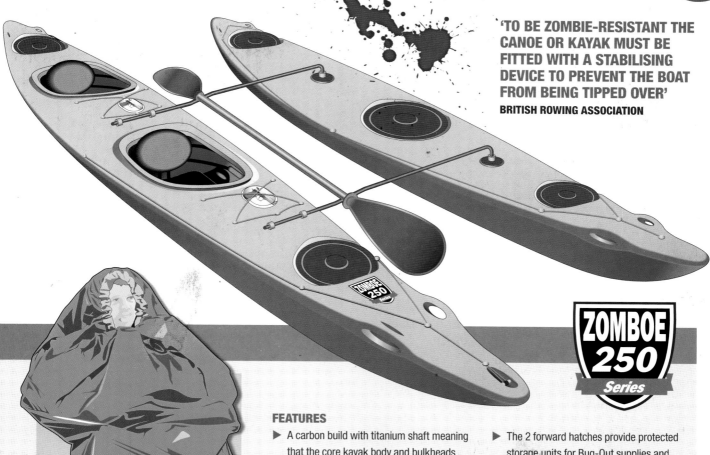

'TO BE ZOMBIE-RESISTANT THE CANOE OR KAYAK MUST BE FITTED WITH A STABILISING DEVICE TO PREVENT THE BOAT FROM BEING TIPPED OVER'
BRITISH ROWING ASSOCIATION

ZOMBOE 250 Series

IN-BUILT SURVIVAL BAG

Strong, lightweight survival bag designed to reduce rapid heat loss and the risk of hypothermia in emergency situations. It is made of heavy-duty polyethylene, is highly scratch resistant, and is coated in an anti-zombie chemical deterrent.

FEATURES

▶ A carbon build with titanium shaft meaning that the core kayak body and bulkheads are virtually indestructible. There is a lightweight aluminium outrigger beam connecting the main body to the float stabiliser (secondary hull).

▶ A specially designed seat and cockpit arrangement, with waterproof side arm pouch and reinforced hip and knee bracers – all designed for long-distance travel and use.

▶ Concealed front and rear flotation bags in both hulls, which are sculpted into the boat providing room for 6 watertight storage wells, plus an additional concealed unit by the side of the cockpit.

▶ All boats in the kayak range have a unique double-fin skeg underneath which further stabilises the boat and makes it easy to direct.

▶ The 3 wells on the main float include an in-built mini water purification unit and water-cooling storage unit.

▶ The 2 forward hatches provide protected storage units for Bug-Out supplies and an in-built survival pack comes with the range. The rear hatch on the main hull is armoured and is designed for ammunition and small firearms.

▶ The anti-zombie marine paint is designed to both camouflage the vessel when on the water and the manufacturers insist that the chemical composition of the paint repels zombies although this fact has not been verified by the Ministry of Zombies.

▶ Each boat in the Zomboe 150 and 250 series comes with 2 high-performance Seattle Sports carbon-fibre shaft 'battle' kayak paddles. Unlike standard paddles, these are designed to stand up to the abuse of endless paddling and whacking the occasional zombie in the water. Durable, efficient and impact-resistant – it's no surprise that these paddles have twice been voted 'Apocalypse Paddle of the Year' by *Survivor Weekly* magazine.

TRAVELLING BY AIR

Escaping the zombies by air has long been the preserve of those rich enough to own personal jets or private light aircraft but things are changing. For the first time, there are airborne options for the average zombie prepper.

In general, zombies and air transport don't mix well at all. Consider Heathrow airport on a bank holiday when the schools are out and seemingly everyone in the UK is simultaneously trying to check their over-sized luggage in. Into this, hurl a zombie outbreak with a few hundred ghouls running wild and the result makes major airports one of the worst places to be during the zombie apocalypse. Equally, a zombie outbreak actually on board a plane will leave most survivors scratching their heads thinking, what the hell can you do in such a confined space? Well, in this section, we'll review air travel as an option in your Bug-Out Plans, and whilst it's true that you're unlikely to be able to pick up a cheap no-frills flight to safety in the sun, thanks to advances in technology, particularly in experimental ultra-light aircraft such as the Xtreme Survivor range from World Gyrocopters, air travel is now becoming a practical alternative.

BUGGING-OUT BY AIR

Most of those serious about their zombie apocalypse transportation will discount major airports and air travel from their Bug-Out Plans. However, as has been mentioned, there are still some useful options out there. It's worth remembering that most airborne Bug-Out Vehicles come with hefty price tags as well as sizeable training and maintenance costs.

The average zombie survivalist on a modest budget should certainly consider their airborne options. Gaining a pilot's licence, getting to know smaller local airports or exploring the potential of the new breed of gyrocopters are all reasonable tasks as you develop your Zombie Survival Plan. Carefully think through your Bug-Out Plans before you make any major commitments. For example, if you're planning a one-way trip to the wilderness with yourself, your family and Bug-Out Supplies, then investing in reasonable airborne transportation may be a viable option.

OPTION 1
SMALL RECREATIONAL AIRCRAFT

PROS

▶ According to the Light Aircraft Association, owning, maintaining and training on a smaller plane is no longer the preserve of the super-rich with options available for most budgets.

▶ There are over 50 commercial airports throughout the country, each with machines and training opportunities.

▶ The planes themselves require shorter runways than larger jets but can still evacuate a reasonable sized party and supplies.

CONS

▶ Although it is now cheaper, it's still a substantial cost – for example, £30,000 will get you a reasonable used plane but then you have all of the other costs...

▶ Ideally, you'd need to be very near your plane when the crisis hits. Even local airports are bound to become dicey once the zombies arrive.

OPTION 2
HELICOPTERS

PROS

▶ Shares many of the same benefits as smaller aircraft although lessons can still set you back hundreds of pounds per hour.

▶ Helicopters are far more flexible due to their unique vertical take-off and landing ability. It is therefore feasible for one or some of your party to guard the chopper when it is put down close to your home to pick up the rest of the survivors and supplies.

CONS

▶ Budget again – Bugging-Out by chopper won't be cheap unless you happen to chance upon a machine and a trained pilot who has nothing better to do.

▶ Most choppers are noisy and that's a big drawback as landing anywhere will attract every unsavoury bandit in the local area, keen to get their grubby hands on your transport and supplies.

TRAVELLING BY AIR
PERSONAL JET PACKS

Personal jet pack travel was the great hope of zombie survivalists in the 1960s with the early preppers dreaming of flying to safety at the press of a booster button. Survivors with a quality jet pack hoped that they could repeat their air escape multiple times, enabling them to use 'air hop' across the rooftops, keeping well away from any zombies and the infected.

That was the dream but in reality personal jet or rocket-propelled transport has never lived up to its billing. It's dangerous, unreliable and expensive. Not a good combination. There has been some useful work done around jet-propelled personal devices but much of it by unlicensed companies looking to cash in on the technology released by NASA in early 2001.

More recently, the jet pack market has been flooded with rogue units, many of which are ineffective and even lethal. With little or no concern for user safety, using one of these cheaply made units is like strapping a leaky propane gas cylinder to your back then lighting it – not recommended.

OPTION 3
ULTRA-LIGHT AIRCRAFT

PROS
► Ultra-light aircraft like gyrocopters and microlights have never been more accessible. There are hundreds of clubs and courses throughout the country.
► Whilst specialist machines like the Xtreme Survivor 100Z range are expensive, you can get a decent second-hand machine for under £10,000.
► Many machines now have robust multi-fuel engines. You can't quite put anything in the tanks but fuel is certainly not such an issue for these aircraft.

CONS
► If you keep your aircraft in the garden or close to your home, it's a real challenge to keep things quiet from neighbours. Remember that friendly person down the road could turn into a desperate knife-wielding lunatic demanding that you take them with you.
► Most machines have limited space for people and supplies, with strict weight limitations.

OPTION 4
AIR BALLOONS AND BLIMPS

PROS
► Massive advances have been made in this field of air transport in recent years, with successful circumnavigations and altitude challenges.
► Many options, particularly hot air or helium balloons are virtually silent so why not combine your desperate Bug-Out escape with some delightful views of the burning remains of civilisation. Ensure that you pack a picnic basket.

CONS
► Hard to find, unreliable and requiring substantial ground support means that currently air balloons and blimps are the stuff of fantasy for serious zombie survivalists.
► The uncontrollable nature of air balloons could see you coming down in a field of zombies. Blimps are better equipped but equally impractical for all but a few qualified experts.

TRAVELLING BY AIR

AIRPORTS AND ZOMBIES

For many, the idea of flying to some safe zone is the perfect escape route from a zombie apocalypse but in reality, unless you have a private plane on a guarded private air strip, the chances are if you try to make it to the nearest airport, you'll either be caught by a deadly rush of survivors, all clambering to get on flights which have long-since been cancelled, or you'll end up stuck in bumper to bumper traffic miles from the terminal. Basically, major airports are no-go areas once the dead show up.

In 2016, the Civil Aviation Authority produced a detailed assessment of the resilience of the UK's airports and air travel infrastructure. The document listed 'viral incident' – a codeword for zombie outbreak often used in official documentation – as the second most imminent threat to the UK's air travel network. There is no doubt that our brave armed response units will put up a good fight against the infected but the report left zombie preppers in no doubt – 'The UK airport network is extremely vulnerable to any viral incidents, particularly where such incidents involve violent and cannibalistic symptoms.' Civil Aviation Authority UK Preparedness Report, March 2016. Bureaucratic jargon which roughly translates as if we have a major zombie outbreak at an airport, jumbo jet will mean jumbo human buffet for the dead.

▶ ZOMBIES ON A PLANE

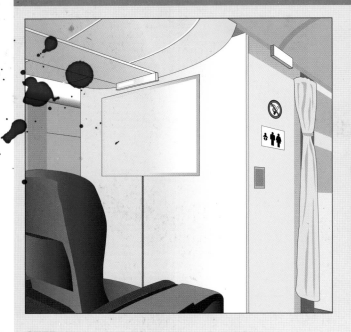

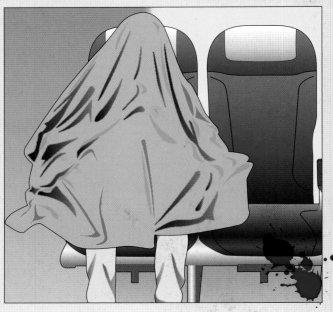

STEP 1
ASSESS THE RISK

Once you're aware of the warning signs, keep an eye out for those with flu-like symptoms. Always select a seat close to the front or back of the plane, if possible close to the WC and kitchen area. Report any symptoms to staff as soon as possible. All air crew and support staff are trained to spot symptoms of the zombic condition.

STEP 2
MAKE YOUR MOVE

If the worst happens and you see someone 'on the turn', it is vital you make your move quickly. Quietly, get as far away as you can – the best location is towards the front of the plane. With very few items available on board as weapons, grab any jumpers or coats you can to at least provide some protection. Blankets can also be used to hurl over infected individuals.

TRAVELLING BY AIR
AIR TRAVEL Q&A

In 2017, the Ministry of Zombies sponsored a series of radio helpline slots on national radio as part of its 'Zombie Defence in the Community' programme. One show focused exclusively on air travel and the questions and answers below may help illuminate some of the key challenges and misunderstandings about Bugging-Out by air.

IF I ALREADY HAVE A TICKET AND GET TO THE AIRPORT, WILL THE AIRLINE HONOUR MY TICKET?
It is unlikely that you'll be able to get in the door at the airport. Expect cancelled flights, heaving crowds and riots. The fact that you have a ticket to somewhere won't make that much difference.

WILL A ZOMBIE APOCALYPSE AFFECT THE AMOUNT OF LUGGAGE I CAN TAKE ON BOARD? I FEEL THAT 20 KGS IS TOO RESTRICTIVE.
Are you serious? We're talking about getting on alive not whether you can afford to take your cricket whites on a summer holiday. You really should read up on the impact of a major zombie outbreak!

WILL I BE ABLE TO USE AIR MILES TO FUND MY ESCAPE BY AIR?
Your air miles are unlikely to buy you an escape route. You may as well change your name to 'Cheap Meat Snack' as far as the zombies are concerned. Can we get rid of this caller?

And so, like a poorly thought through forum discussion on Reddit, the phone-in slot descended into chaos. Clearly, the general public weren't ready for an open discussion on the threat posed by the walking dead.

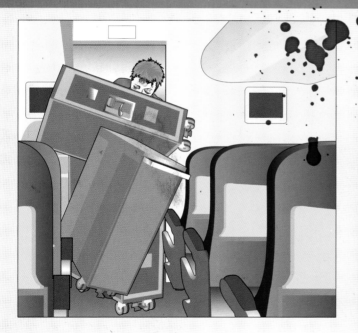

STEP 3
CONTAINMENT

Join any like-minded survivors in containing the infected area. Barricade off a section of the plane using items such as luggage or catering carts. You'll need to be ruthless as there will doubtless be some living trapped outside but do your best to help them. Let the pilot team, who will be securely sealed off in the front, deal with getting the aircraft to safety.

STEP 4
CONTAINMENT FAILURE

If your containment fails, grab water, food and any uninflated lifejackets and lock yourself in one of the toilets. You can assume the pilots are still safely locked in the cockpit but if the plane starts to behave erratically and you fear a crash landing, inflate the life jackets around you to create a protective cocoon... It's your best chance of surviving.

TRAVELLING BY AIR

BUGGING-OUT BY GYROCOPTER

So you've decided that the gyrocopter is the right option for Bugging-Out – there is certainly plenty of choice out there on the market, including the 100Z range profiled here – but before you buy a leather flying jacket and consider which shades to wear to get that ultimate pilot look, there are some things to consider – in addition, of course, to the major decision about what machine to buy.

▶ Get all the training and practice you can before Z-Day arrives. Get qualified with the right pilot's licence then get plenty of hours in the air. The more skilled a pilot you are, the better the chances that you will reach your Bug-Out Location.

▶ Plan your Bug-Out Route carefully; assume that any GPS technology will be down. Learn to navigate by landmarks. One of the simplest ways is to use our motorways to guide you. If you can, complete an entire practice run. Try starting at night if you are experienced enough.

▶ Keep your machine as discreetly as possible. Some preppers buy two machines, keeping one at the airfield, and one hidden nearer to their home. Not everyone has that kind of budget but ensure that your machine is hidden and accessible in a crisis. The ideal set up would include a runway area close to home, even if it's just a field at the end of the garden.

▶ Watch the weight on your machine. Get the balance of supplies right as an over-weight gyrocopter could get you killed. Know the tolerances of your plane and be cautious about who is coming with you. If you have room for 1 plus your Bug-Out Supplies then don't be tempted to squeeze another desperate survivor on board if you only have a 2-seater.

▶ Scout your long-term Bug-Out Location carefully. If possible, hide extra fuel and supplies on site. Always have a back up location and check out potential stop off points if it's going to be a longer journey.

TRAVELLING BY AIR
LANDING GUIDELINES

Most of your flight training will take place on a structured flight programme and your tutors may or may not be aware of your zombie Bug-Out Plans. Much of what you learn will be relevant but you should also be aware of the particular challenges a zombie apocalypse will bring. Remember, if you don't know an area always assume it is hostile. One drawback of a gyrocopter is that below a certain height, the noise can attract unwanted attention from both the living and the dead.

FOUR STEP PROCESS FOR LANDING

1 Complete an eyeball and sensor scan of the area. Check out any principle landmarks and identify a safe landing zone.

2 Drop a synthetic meat bomb a few miles away to draw off any zombie hordes in the area.

3 Pop a smoke bomb down at a similar location, it can distract hostile bandits into thinking survivors are in that location.

4 Once on the ground, complete a further eye ball and sensor scan. Always be ready to get out of Dodge as soon as possible if required.

► XTREME SURVIVOR 100Z GYROCOPTER

What if there was a relatively cheap experimental flying machine available? What if it needed only very basic training and a bit of open space to take off? Well, the Xtreme Survivor range from World Gyrocopters has been developed just to fill this niche in the zombie survival market for an affordable and practical airborne long-range Bug-Out Vehicle.

XTREME SURVIVOR 100Z GYROCOPTER

World Gyrocopters, Lydd Airport, Kent

LOCATION

Over 100 models sold, so all over the world. Showroom in Lydd, Kent.

PURPOSE

A high-performance ultra-light aircraft designed especially for post-apocalyptic use as a Bug-Out Vehicle.

CREW

Available in solo, twin-seater or quad-seat configurations.

TECHNICAL SPECIFICATIONS

Air framework in high-grade stainless steel, electro 'walking dead' polished. Tinted zombie-proof plexiglass windscreens, front and side. All aluminium welded 30 gallon fuel cell. Apocalypse IP 360 Engine, 225 hp with mounted fuel pump and super-filters. Military-grade main landing gear. High-performance rotor system with 80 inch carbon fibre blades.

ARMAMENTS

Standard model is unarmed but has fixing points for a door-mounted machine gun and under-carriage anti-zombie chaff-missile pods as well as a host of other features to help the pilot combat the undead, such as the refrigerated 'meat bomb', which drops hunks of synthetic human flesh designed to attract zombies to a particular location, and the revolutionary 'Cool Body Sensor' system, which uses a special form of infra-red heat sensing camera to detect movement and the lower body temperature of a zombie.

USAGE GUIDELINES

Airborne Bugging-Out is the dream of many zombie preppers and this range of British-made gyrocopters makes it possible. The 2-seater version needs a maximum of 100 metres for take-off but only 20 metres for landing and with a maximum range of 400 miles on the standard version, once you are prepped with your vehicle, start planning your perfect Bug-Out Location. Preppers tend to recommend the twin-seater version as it has significantly more stowage space.

RANGE

With the extended 30 gallon fuel tank plus additional apocalypse-grade drop tank of 15 gallons, the twin-seat 100Z range can comfortably cover up to 400 miles fully loaded at an average cruise speed of around 80 mph at 10,000 feet.

BUDGET

Base model Xtreme Survivor 100Z Gyrocopter is £45,000 plus transportation. Comes with anti-zombie features as standard. The Xtreme Survivor 200Z Gyrocopter is the 4-seater version and is custom built to order – most units costing around £80,000.

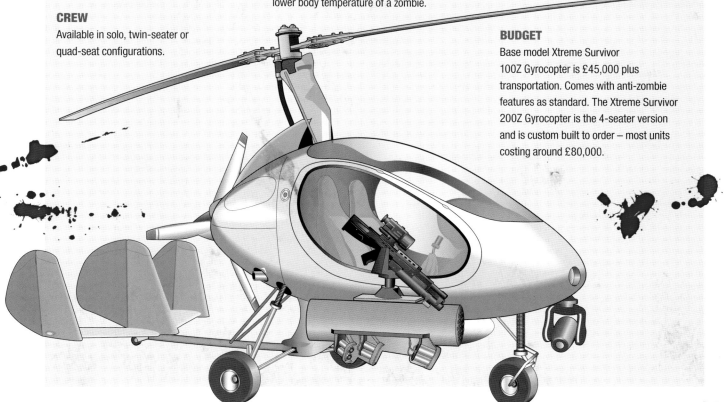

© Sean T. Page

No part of this publication may be reproduced, stored in a retrieval system or transmitted, in any form or by any means, electronic, mechanical, photocopying, recording or otherwise, without prior permission in writing from the publisher.

First published in November 2017

A catalogue record for this book is available from the British Library

ISBN 978 1 78521 166 9

Library of Congress catalog card no. 2017949597

Haynes Publishing, Sparkford, Yeovil, Somerset BA22 7JJ, UK
Tel: +44 1963 440635
Website: www.haynes.com

Haynes North America, Inc.,
861 Lawrence Drive, Newbury Park, California 91320, USA

Printed and bound in Malaysia

Author	Sean T. Page
Illustrator	Ian Moores
Editor	Louise McIntyre
Designer	Richard Parsons

AUTHOR'S ACKNOWLEDGEMENTS

There were many experts involved in this book and I would like to particularly thank Steve 'Rusty' Langdon for answering endless questions about his wasteland scooter and his war stories. To Mrs Eileen Cassidy, for travelling to London on several occasions and for allowing us to print plans to her apocalypse shopping trolley. To Toyota, Honda, Hyundai and the RAC, who provided some of the motoring inspiration for this volume. To all the survivors who kindly contributed their vehicle plans and case studies for inclusion – we couldn't fit them all in but they all proved to be invaluable to our research. Finally, to my partners in crime – Ian, Louise and Richard – for their belief that such a book is essential to help protect the country and for settling the regrettable incident with the flame thrower out of court. Above all, to my wife Constance and daughter Nikita, who is currently converting her trike into a devastating wasteland cruiser.